ANGELA M. SANDERS

Head Case

WIDOW'S KISS

Printed in the United States of America.

First Printing, 2018

ISBN 978-0-9904133-9-4

Widow's Kiss
P.O. Box 82488
Portland, OR 97282

www.WidowsKissBooks.com

Book design: Eric Lancaster

To the Cargo Girls

Head
Case

Chapter 1

Joanna had once heard that everything you need to know about a man you learn on the first date. She was married now, and first dates were a thing of her past. But she believed the same principle applied to houses. Within five minutes of being in someone's home, she knew the person's essential character. For a vintage clothing shop owner like her, it was almost as good as rummaging through their closets.

A glance at Bradley Stroden's house told her he was meticulous. A buttercup-yellow tower rose from the Victorian mansion, and urns of neatly trimmed roses managed to remain crisp even in the August heat. From the house's location on a bluff lording over the Willamette River and the snarl of traffic siphoning off the interstate freeway, Stroden clearly kept himself apart from the rest of the world. The leopard print curtain lining peeking from the windows showed that, style-wise, he followed his own star.

What kind of clothing did he have for sale? She let her mind wander to flapper's dresses and long, bias-cut evening gowns.

Joanna reined in her expectations when a man in his twenties with Elvis-styled sideburns, jeans, and a vintage Jackals T-shirt answered the door.

He stuck out a hand. "Hi. You're from Tallulah's Closet?"

She nodded. Her dreams fell to ash. This guy probably had a few old concert T-shirts and Mom's mink coat—secondhand fur was tough to sell—and thought he'd make a bundle.

"Joanna Hayworth," she said. "You must be Mr. Stroden."

He laughed. "No, his secretary, Luke. Pleased to meet you. Come in. I set out the things Mr. Stroden wants to sell."

Heartened, Joanna followed him down the oak-floored hall with its peacock print wallpaper, through a dining area with blinds drawn, to a sun-filled room in the house's back corner.

Luke had set up a clothing rack, unusual in a private sale, unless an estate sale company handled it. Linen wardrobe bags lined its rod. Usually she had to paw through stacks of dresses slumped over a sofa or piled on a bed, or, worse, was left with garbage sacks of clothing that still stank of their long-dead owners. Here, every surface shone, and the air smelled floral. Joanna breathed in. Yes, like violets.

"Help yourself," Luke said. "The dresses are on this side, and the suits and coats are over there. I didn't know if you bought accessories, but Mr. Stroden set aside a few things that might catch your interest." He pointed to hat and shoe boxes on the table.

"Would you like a cup of tea?" An older woman stood in the doorway. Instead of the short, practical hair many women her age wore, her hair fell in white ringlets to her shoulders, giving her a girlish look. On the sideboard, she set a vase of late summer roses threaded with marigolds and golden zinnias.

Joanna glanced at Luke, then again at the woman. Heck, if Stroden had a secretary, why not a housekeeper, too? She was dressed like one, complete with apron. "No, thank you."

"Mr. Stroden loves clothing. He used to be a wardrobe assistant in Hollywood." Luke lowered his voice. "For Edith Head."

Joanna lifted her eyebrows. "These are movie costumes?"

Luke pulled out a balloon-backed chair and sat. "Oh, no. That was during the fifties. After a few years, he moved back up to Portland into the old family house. Here."

"No kidding. You're sure he doesn't have any of his work with Edith Head squirreled away?"

Luke laughed. "If he does, don't you think he'd take them to Sotheby's?"

"He must have some great stories."

"Definitely. That's why I'm here, actually. I'm helping with his memoir."

"A memoir from a Hollywood costume designer? I'd definitely read that." Joanna turned to the clothing rack. "These must be his wife's clothes, then."

He shook his head. "He never married. When he came back to Portland, he took up a job illustrating ads. Those days, when a department store, say, Meier and Frank, wanted clothing sketched for an ad, they brought it to his studio. Sometimes he held onto the outfits, and that's what we have here. Go ahead, take a look."

Joanna's mind was still with Hollywood. What she'd give to get her hands on one of those costumes. Some of the beauty of a vintage dress was its construction and materials, usually worlds above the cheap stuff made today, but a good part of it was the dress's story, too. She could hold a 1940s suit by the jacket's shoulders and imagine a whole world of seamed stockings, rounded sedans, and lunch counters. Add a Hollywood movie set to the mix, and the daydreams quadrupled.

"I know that look. You're thinking of the movies, aren't you?" Another voice came from the doorway, but this was the voice of an older man. He wore a satin-finished burgundy smoking jacket wrapped over wool pants. Despite the lounging attire, his hair was brilliantined into a style that would have made Clark Gable envious. And now the scent of violets was stronger.

Joanna smiled. "I admit it. I was. You must be Mr. Stroden. I'm Joanna."

Up close, his skin was as dewy as a nine-year-old's. He didn't hide his head-to-toe assessment of Joanna. She smoothed the 1940s rayon over her knees. Good thing she'd chosen an offbeat print of bluebirds for this morning's appointment. The dress's cut was good, too, with a peplum at the waist and a twist at the collar. She'd kept the outfit from going cartoonishly retro with modern red slingback sandals.

"Pardon my informal dress," he said. "I'm afraid I'm a late riser."

Luke was now on his feet. "Are you ready for your coffee, Mr. Stroden?"

"I'll be in the dressing room. Oh, and bring two cups."

Luke cocked his head. Something in Stroden's reply had surprised him.

Stroden's Turkish slippers tapped on the parquet floor as he disappeared into the next room. Joanna's heart beat strangely, as if she'd just seen someone step from a film into real life, then vanish again as mysteriously.

"Joanna?" Stroden reappeared in the doorway.

"Yes?" Her voice came out a whisper.

"Aren't you coming? You want to see my work with Ms. Head, don't you?"

*⁎⁎

Joanna's pulse rocketed from calm to happy jig as she followed Bradley Stroden up the stairs that curved at the rear of the entry hall.

For a man who might have held AARP membership for thirty-plus years, he climbed surely and steadily, one hand light on the polished banister. His posture was ramrod straight. The crazy idea crossed her mind that he wore a corset under the smoking jacket.

"In here." He opened a door to what looked to have once been a dressing room to the bedroom next door. Amplified by the summer heat, the scent of violets was even stronger here.

Stroden crossed the room and raised the blinds. "Have a seat, Ms. Hayworth."

"Joanna, please." Two petit point-embroidered chairs flanked a small round table.

"I'm sorry to interrupt your business downstairs. Luke was helpful?"

"Yes," she said, taking in the art glass lamp with its bronze base and the jewel-toned rug.

"When we're finished, he'll show you the items we're selling. But I thought, given your profession, you might be interested in a few of the pieces I won't be letting go of."

"From Edith Head?"

"Here he is now. Luke, you can put the tray there."

Luke set a silver tray with an antique violet-sprigged porcelain coffeepot on the table and, surprisingly, two contemporary coffee cups in a space age design. He placed an oval tin of Flavigny pastilles next to Stroden's coffee cup. Violets adorned the lid. "Your new shipment came in this morning's mail."

"They must have changed the packaging." Stroden lifted the tin. "Thank you, Luke. I'll send Joanna to you in a few minutes, and we can resume dictation in an hour or so."

"I'll see if Mary Pat needs my help in the kitchen." Luke's steps tripped lightly down the hall.

"Let's take our coffee off the tray. It's barbaric to be served directly from a tray, don't you agree?" Stroden said.

"I can't think that anything about this coffee is barbaric." Distracted, Joanna doctored hers with cream. The wardrobe doors were still firmly shut, but in her mind, fluffs of silk chiffon and crisply tailored suits filled the racks behind them.

"Yes, I worked with Edith Head," Stroden said. He tipped his head back and his eyes flickered shut, as if he'd told this story a hundred times. "Not that I did that much. I was a good sketch artist, and I learned to mimic Edie's style." He opened an eye and turned to her. "Of course, her style was a double of Travis Banton's, her mentor. That was at the end of the forties and up to the mid-fifties."

"So, you must have worked with some big stars. Did you ever meet Barbara Stanwyck? I watched *The Lady Eve* again just last night." The coffee was rich and smooth. Stroden didn't mess around with subpar aesthetic experiences. Her gaze was pulled again to the wardrobe doors.

He nodded. "That movie was before my time, but Barbara was delightful. Some of the other actresses weren't quite as charming. Joan Crawford's antics are legend, of course."

"I can imagine."

"When she came in for fittings, she refused to let anyone else use the bathroom. Even Edie. We all had to run to the next building to take care of business. I learned to check the schedule and watch my coffee intake."

"Joan Crawford must have been modest."

"Modest?" Stroden burst into laughter. "That's a good one. She used to parade naked in the dressing room. She didn't care who else was there." He smiled, as if remembering a particularly choice story.

"But she wasn't the only diva with a foul temper."

"Oh?"

His chin barely nodded. "You'll have to read my memoir to find out more."

"I will, believe me. It all sounds so magical. Tell me about Edith Head. She had so much style."

"She had to. Fact is, Edie somewhat resembled a rat."

"A rat?" Joanna set down her coffee cup.

"I know what you're thinking, but Edie would have agreed with me. She knew fashion was not for her. She chose style, instead, a direction many more people should consider. She dressed for her character: opinionated and autocratic, yet she knew which derrières to kiss."

"You make her out as a sort of Hollywood Rasputin."

He pursed his lips. "Not bad. I may put that in my memoir, if you don't mind. Unfortunately, she limited her written remembrances to whitewashed fashion anecdotes. She had a bead on Hollywood that left Hedda Hopper in the dust." He toyed with the tin of pastilles. "How's the coffee?"

"Delicious, thank you." She'd barely touched it. She didn't want to miss a word of Stroden's conversation.

"Edie's style was marvelous as far as it went. She dressed perfectly for her job — chic enough to impress her clients, yet unthreatening. At home, she wore Mexican blouses and ethnic jewelry — all simple and bold. But evening looks"— he shook his head —"she never did figure out how to negotiate black tie."

"Amazing. It must have been hard to leave all that and come back to Portland."

"Hollywood is a young man's game. At some point, we all move on. A few of us have even settled here. You've heard of Callie Rampton?

The actress?"

Joanna shook her head. "What was she in?"

"B movies mostly. She was a popular best friend or secretary. She had steady work until, well, never mind." The saucer clinked as he lifted his cup. For a moment, he seemed to be weighing whether to tell her something. Finally, he said, "The year I left, I'd worked on a film. *Starlit Wonder*, it was called."

Starlit Wonder. Didn't sound familiar. Joanna had watched every movie from Hollywood's Golden Age that the local video store carried and had driven to Movie Madness to rent the rest of them. She kept two VCRs from the thrift store on back-up just to make sure she could watch films that had never made it to DVD.

"I haven't seen that one," she said.

"No one has. It was never released. It got as far as a final edit — score and all — but the producer pulled it."

"And the studio let him? Why?"

Stroden smiled. "Money talks, naturally. But scandal screams. The story of *Starlit Wonder* is my memoir's centerpiece." Once again, he rested his head back and closed his eyes. "The stories. You wouldn't believe the stories. You'll have to wait to read the rest. You and a few other interested parties."

Joanna bet Stroden hadn't been a studio worker who slaved during the day and returned home to card games in his Spanish-style apartment building at night. He'd been out at parties, looking, listening, and taking in scenes of drunken starlets and adulterous studio executives. He would have measured the quality of their stemware and cut of their jackets, and he would have soaked up their stories. Now he was telling them.

"I won't live forever," he said. "Frankly, with the way I've conducted myself, I'm surprised I've made it this long." He tapped his head. "I don't want to take this with me. A few more weeks with Luke, and I should be through the best years. Including *Starlit Wonder*. That's the film these costumes are from."

"You know something you're not telling," Joanna said. She longed to crack the window just a bit to thin the stuffy floral air. Shelley's "Odors, when sweet violets sicken, live within the sense they quicken," a poem she'd memorized in high school, came to her mind unbidden.

He reached for the tin of pastilles. "Would you like one? They're a habit for me, I'm afraid."

"No, thank you." No more violets.

"I have them sent from France. Take one." He set a sugar-dusted candy on her saucer and slipped another between his lips. "No, I can't tell you more about *Starlit Wonder*. Not yet. But I did keep a few prime bits of the wardrobe." A sly smile stretched his baby-smooth skin. "Would you like to see?"

"Please." She pushed away the coffee cup.

Stroden rose and took a step toward the wardrobe. Just one step. He turned, and his eyes widened, as if he saw something horrible behind her. He clutched his chest and his mouth hardened into a grimace.

Joanna leapt to her feet. "Mr. Stroden!"

He choked as if he were trying to say something, but only a queer whistling noise escaped his throat.

"Luke!" Joanna yelled down the hall. "Call 9-1-1! I think Mr. Stroden's having a heart attack!"

Legs crumpling, back stiff, Stroden fell to the rug.

Joanna knelt and shook his shoulders. "Mr. Stroden! Bradley!"

It wasn't Luke who'd answered Joanna's shout, but the housekeeper.

Stunned, she moved to Stroden's chair and sat, frozen.

"Do you have a phone? We need to call an ambulance," Joanna said.

"He's dead," she whispered.

"I don't have a cell phone," Joanna repeated. "We need to call 9-1-1."

Luke arrived, gasping, at the door. "What happened?"

"Call an ambulance. *Now*. Mr. Stroden collapsed." How many times did she have to repeat it? She tipped up Stroden's chin and listened for his breath. Nothing. She racked her memory for how to perform CPR.

Luke tossed his phone to the table and knelt beside her. "They're on their way."

Stroden lay limp on his back. His trousers maintained their knifepoint pleat even now, and the silk smoking jacket gleamed in the morning light. He would have been gratified to show sartorial splendor to the end, she thought. If this was, indeed, the end.

Chapter 2

Joanna watched from the street as the ambulance backed out of the driveway and sped up the boulevard, switching on its siren as it merged into traffic. The siren's wail was a welcome note of hope.

She and Luke had alternated pressing Stroden's chest until the paramedics had arrived and taken over. At that point, she'd become an intrusion and let herself out of the Victorian house — down the curving staircase, through the wide entry hall with its central table and pot of violets, and out the double doors.

A motion from a window next door drew her attention. The neighbor's curtains flickered, and a woman's face appeared briefly in the window before the curtain dropped. She'd have lots to gossip about at the grocery store this afternoon. Old Blue's engine grumbled as usual as Joanna started the aging Corolla. She drove the few miles home in a daze. Underlying the daze stirred a vague excitement.

It was testament to her distraction that she didn't even wince when she heard the soundtrack of a made-for-TV movie coming from the basement. Her husband's uncle Gene had been living with them since their honeymoon, when he'd housesat for them. He'd asked if they minded if he stayed "a few days" after they returned home while he "looked for a permanent situation." Unless this permanent situation appeared on TV or in the mysterious places he disappeared to at night, Uncle Gene would be living with them forever. In a rambling mansion like Bradley Stroden's, that might have been okay. In Joanna's modest two-bedroom bungalow, the bathroom practically needed its own full-time scheduler.

What she really wanted to do was discuss the morning with the portrait of a tight-lipped matron she'd long ago dubbed Aunt Vanderburgh. She'd found Auntie V at Goodwill, the angle of the portrait's brows over horn-rimmed glasses making it clear Auntie V didn't approve of the amateur seascapes and faded Jesus prints stacked around her. Auntie V had been her confidante for years. Marriage, and now Uncle Gene, had uprooted Joanna's usual survival techniques.

"Joanna, is that you? Want help bringing in clothes?"

She tossed her purse on the chaise longue by the front window and rubbed the back of her hands. They still ached from giving CPR, and the back of one wrist was beginning to bruise. "No clothes to bring in today, but thanks."

The television's laugh track disappeared, and footsteps sounded on the stairs. "Nothing worth buying, huh?" Gene asked.

Uncle Gene was an unexpected combination of Portland's plaid-wearing working class and a dinner club dancer's elegance. He'd mentored Paul in becoming a woodworker specializing in preservation techniques, but at night he'd robbed houses. That was in the past, though. Or so he said. He swore he'd been clean since his recent stint in prison.

"No. No dresses this time," Joanna said, still dazed. "What have you been up to today?"

"Checked in with my parole officer this morning. Later, I thought I might help Paul with the cabinets he's working on."

This was a sore spot with Paul. He couldn't take his uncle with him to job sites—most clients didn't look favorably on having a felon on site, no matter how keen his ability to turn a lathe. Yet the alternative was hours in front of the television, unless Paul had projects in his shop. As a result, he'd started bringing work home just to keep Gene busy, even though it cost more time than it saved.

"No leads on jobs?" Joanna couldn't help adding.

"Jo, what's wrong?"

She slumped into a dining room chair. "I saw someone collapse this morning. Maybe die."

Gene took the chair nearest hers. "You what?"

"The whole situation was surreal." She forced herself to breathe deeply. "We called the paramedics and did CPR. I hope he's okay."

"I'm sorry, honey. This was the house sale you visited this morning?"

"Uh huh. Did you ever know a fashion illustrator named Bradley Stroden?" They were both longtime Portlanders. It wasn't impossible they'd crossed paths.

Recognition flickered over his face, but disappeared as quickly as it had surfaced. "Stroden, you say?"

"You know him, don't you? Maybe professionally?"

He examined a fingernail before replying. "He lives in the yellow Victorian overlooking the Ross Island Bridge, right? The one with the tower?"

"That's him."

"I plead the fifth. But rumor has it he kept a Deco sterling Tiffany tea set that wasn't getting the love it deserved. Stroden collapsed, did he?"

"Right in front of me. One moment we're having coffee and he's getting ready to show me some costumes Edith Head designed, and the next he's convulsing on the floor."

"Heart attack, sounds like."

She remembered the violet pastilles and how Stroden had clutched his chest. "Maybe."

"Honey, I'm sorry. Is there anything I can do for you?"

She placed her hand on his. "No, but thank you." It might test her patience sometimes to have such a full house, but Gene was a sweet guy. "I think I'll head over to Tallulah's Closet. Could you help me take down the portrait hanging in my office?"

If home wasn't the respite it had been for Joanna, Tallulah's Closet still set her mind right. These days, it was the one space she could control, and over the years she'd transformed it into her fantasy of a starlet's dressing room, complete with flowers, animal print furnishings, and gilded mirrors.

She lugged the portrait of Auntie V through the shop's door. Beyond the mannequins, dressed today in summery pastels, Joanna's best friend and coworker, Apple, was seated at the tiki bar that served as the shop's cashier counter, rubbing with unusual vigor at the scuffs on a pair of alligator stiletto pumps. Today, Apple wore her favorite Zandra Rhodes caftan and looked more than usual like a Rolling Stones groupie in Marrakech.

"How are things here?" Joanna asked.

"Gavin called again." Apple was going through a contentious separation with her husband. "But I don't want to talk about it right now."

"You're sure?"

She glanced at the portrait of Auntie V. "Definitely. Not even to her. How was the haunted house? Anything good?"

"Haunted house." Embracing the comfort of the familiar, Joanna leaned the painting on the tiki bar. She lifted her porcelain mug from behind the counter, just as she always did, and unscrewed the lid of her thermos to smell the rich coffee. Anything but violets. Her shoulders relaxed. "If it wasn't haunted before, it is now." She told Apple about the morning, from greeting the secretary to almost seeing the Edith Head designs to Bradley Stroden's collapse.

Apple froze as she listened, a pump hovering in the air. "Heart attack?"

"I guess so," Joanna said.

Apple set down the shoe and leaned on her elbow. "But you're not convinced."

"He was getting up there in years. A heart attack isn't out of the question. But just before he died, he'd eaten a violet candy — you should have been there, the whole place smelled like violets — and mentioned that it was different packaging."

"So he could have been poisoned?"

"Poison?" a woman asked.

Joanna and Apple snapped their attention to the customer at the door.

"No poison here. Come in. May I help you?" Joanna said.

"I'm looking for something to wear to a company dinner." The woman, probably in her late twenties, had adopted the L.A. look of yoga pants, T-shirt, and straight, highlighted hair topped with a baseball cap. She was fit but had a boyish figure, and Joanna would have guessed she'd shop for a special occasion at a boutique at the mall that specialized in Lycra and low-cut necklines. A shop with a name like "Slinky's" or "Glamour Babe."

Joanna and Apple exchanged glances. Clearly, they'd come to

the same conclusion. "Did you have anything particular in mind?"

The customer lifted the sleeve of a 1950s houndstooth suit and dropped it. "There's this guy in my office. He really likes Marilyn Monroe. I don't have the figure for that."

Now it was coming together. "Two things," Joanna said. "First, let's talk shape. Not many of us have Marilyn's curves. It looks like you work out. You're strong."

The woman stood straighter. "I do Pilates three times a week."

"But your bra is shot," Apple said. "A Marilyn-style dress requires undergarments that make the most of what you have."

Apple seemed to be going for the tough-love approach. You wouldn't expect it given the caftans and Indian dresses she wore, but she could be a tyrant about foundation wear.

The woman's hands flew to her chest. "This bra was expensive."

"I'm sure it was." Apple smiled reassuringly. "But how old is it? Have you been fitted lately?"

Four out of five women wore old bras that had probably never fit them to begin with. All they wanted was something comfortable. They didn't know that a bra could be both comfortable and fit well. Joanna's clothing was vintage, but her bras were Belgian and brand new. Her underwear, on the other hand, tended to be cotton and came in a multi-pack. Apple didn't have to know about that.

"A good bra costs money, but it will make everything you wear look better," Apple said.

"Absolutely," Joanna said. "We can give you the addresses of a couple of good places to go for a fitting. But I want to get to the second point, the part about Marilyn Monroe."

The woman pulled off her cap. Her hair was thin but silky. "Yeah?"

"What do you think of her style?"

She shifted feet and looked at her hands. "She's sexy, I guess."

"What's your favorite dress of hers?" Apple asked.

Joanna flashed her a smile. Clever approach.

"I don't know. I guess the one where she's standing over the subway grate."

She probably couldn't remember another dress Monroe wore. Which proved she didn't really crave Monroe's look. And, frankly, her figure and the hint of style she showed nudged Joanna in another direction.

"What do you think of Ali McGraw?" Joanna asked.

"Or Lauren Hutton?" Apple added.

The woman's face lit up. "They're so natural, but strong. Remember the girl in the old ads for Charlie perfume? I loved that pantsuit with the wide legs."

"You'd look good in that," Joanna said. Pair a pantsuit with a saddle leather bag and gold hoops, and the customer would look fresh and vibrant enough for a guest appearance on *Charlie's Angels*.

"I always wanted a Gucci purse with the big flap and a horse bit."

Even better. Joanna nodded her approval. "Maybe platform sandals with a tall heel?"

"But mostly flats to run around in," the woman said. Her mind was clearly racing, stocking her closet with tunics and pants in the styles she loved. All at once, she looked up, serious. "But that's not very sexy. I mean, you'd never see Marilyn in a pantsuit."

"What's sexy is embracing your own style, whatever that is. You need to be you." Joanna reached to the rack beyond the customer and pulled out a black and white silk jersey wrap dress. "This is sexy."

"Especially once you get that new bra," Apple added.

"Vintage Diane von Furstenberg. One of her first wrap dresses.

The style that made her famous."

The customer took the satin padded hanger from Joanna and touched the dress's collar. In her mind, she might be walking into the restaurant for the dinner she'd talked about. Her body seemed charged with a special energy. She looked more confident already.

"Can I try it?"

"Definitely. The dressing rooms are back there. Just pull down the curtain. What size shoe do you wear?" Joanna said.

"Nine."

"Here's a pair of 1970s Celine sandals that would go great with it. That way, you'll get the whole effect."

A few minutes later, the woman emerged from the dressing room. She swung her hair over her shoulders and swiveled in front of the mirror. Heels weren't new to her, and she navigated the four-inch sandals with grace. This was one of Joanna's favorite moments — when a customer caught sight of herself in a new way truer to her style — and in the hundreds of times she'd seen it, it never failed to rouse a surge of joy.

"What do you think?" Joanna said.

The customer smoothed her hands over her torso. "I'll take it. Shoes, too. Do you have any more?"

"Those dresses aren't easy to find these days," Apple said. "But I bet we have a few other things you'd like."

"Try a pedicure in copper brown," Joanna added.

An hour later, the customer left with a confident step and two full bags full of clothing wrapped in pink tissue. As for the dinner and the guy who admired Marilyn Monroe, who knew? One thing was for sure. The customer was more likely than ever to go for what she wanted.

"She did look a bit like Ali McGraw," Apple said.

"I wish people would stop wearing exercise clothes in public," Joanna said. "We need more glamour on the streets."

"I hear you. Not that life has to be a movie set, but you have to get dressed. Why not make the most of it?"

They'd had this conversation countless times, but the mention of a "movie set" brought back the morning's scene. Joanna's satisfied glow dimmed.

"You're thinking of the man you saw this morning, aren't you?" Apple asked. Her gaze was long, thoughtful.

"I can't help it. There's one thing in particular that stands out."

"What?" Apple came around the counter.

"Like I said, before he collapsed, he'd eaten a pastille de Flavigny. Violet flavored. Have you ever seen them?"

"The little sugar candies with the anise seed inside, right?"

"Right. What if it was the pastille that killed him and not natural causes?"

"Did you tell the police about the pastille?"

"No. Luke, Stroden's secretary, called an ambulance. As soon as it came, I left. I don't know if the police even showed up. Why would they?"

Apple returned to the alligator pump. "I guess it will depend on what happens at the hospital."

"He was alive when the ambulance left. At least, I think he was—they turned on the siren. Stroden had to be in his eighties. If he doesn't make it…" He'd been so alive, so full of style and stories about old Hollywood. How could he die?

"Yes?"

"If he doesn't make it, maybe they'll simply chalk up his collapse to natural causes and not investigate."

Apple set the pump aside. "So, that's what's worrying you. Just call the hospital — or the police — and tell them about the candy. Let them take it from there."

Yes. It was just a phone call. "I'll do it. After lunch. I need a minute for everything to sink in." She carried Auntie V's portrait to the closet behind the counter and clicked on the light. As she fumbled through a jar of buttons and orphaned earrings for a nail, apprehension stirred in her gut. Something was beginning. Some bottle was uncorked, and she didn't know what would pour out of it.

Outside, the front door's bell chimed. "May I help you?" Apple said in a tone of voice she didn't normally use for customers. Joanna leaned the portrait against the closet's wall and went to the door to listen.

"I'm Lieutenant Roscoe from the Portland Police Bureau. I'd like to speak with Joanna Hayworth."

Joanna stepped out of the closet and couldn't help drawing in her breath. "That's me."

"I understand you saw Bradley Stroden shortly before he died.

Chapter

"He died?" Joanna said.

"He fell into a coma but died soon after reaching the hospital. Yes, Bradley Stroden is dead."

A few months earlier, it might have been Detective Foster Crisp who'd have come to question Joanna, but he'd retired. This new guy, Roscoe, spoke quickly where Crisp would have considered his words. She caught a hint of an East Coast accent. She missed Crisp's cowboy boots, laconic manner, and quick, sharp thinking. Roscoe was middle-aged and short with high-water pants that had likely fit him better before his belly's thrust had yanked them up further. He had a marvelous head of steely curls, though.

"I want to confirm that you were at the Stroden residence when Mr. Stroden collapsed."

"Yes, I was there. I had an appointment at ten o'clock."

"An appointment for what?"

"To buy clothing. I own a vintage clothing boutique." She waved at the racks of dresses. "Do you know what killed him?"

"What makes you so sure it wasn't a natural death?" the detective asked.

A gray-haired woman with a garment bag over her arm entered the store. Apple met her near the door. The woman was likely looking to sell an old wedding dress or her mother's prized evening gown. Apple could handle it.

"You're here, aren't you? A homicide detective?" Joanna said. This guy was beginning to get irritating.

"I asked you a question," Roscoe said.

"Look." The word came out cushioned in air. "Just before he fell, I saw him eat a pastille de Flavigny. Maybe it's silly, but it crossed my mind that it might have been poisoned."

"A what?"

"The violet candies in the tin on the table in Mr. Stroden's dressing room. I saw him take one just before he died."

"Come again?"

Joanna glanced toward the woman with the garment bag. "We don't have much privacy here. I live close by—just a few blocks away. Could we talk there?"

The detective followed her glance to the customer. "I see. Sure, I guess that's fine. Come with me."

They took Roscoe's Crown Victoria to her house and parked in front. As Joanna unlocked the front door, she heard the back door shut. Gene had a second sense for police vehicles, and he clearly didn't plan to stick around.

"Nice place you got." Roscoe glanced at the chaise longue by the front window before choosing the club chair in front of the fireplace. Pepper, Joanna's cat, stuck his black head out from under the chair to sniff at the man's loafers. "Now, suppose you tell me, step by step, what happened this morning."

She closed her eyes and recounted the morning as completely as she remembered it. "Stroden kept hinting at his memoir, how people would be knocked out by its revelations." She opened her eyes. "Could be a motive for murder."

"You're talking murder again."

"Like I said, why else would you be here? If you'd decided his death was natural, that is."

Roscoe nodded as he spoke. "You're right. Stroden's secretary gave us a flash drive with a draft of the memoir on it. And these, um, what did you call them?"

"Pastilles de Flavigny. Violet candies." She couldn't help feeling slightly smug. She'd known something was up.

"You think they were poisoned?"

"They might have been. They'd be worth testing. Mr. Stroden died in his dressing room, upstairs," Joanna said.

"Yes."

She pictured the hall's green and purple Persian carpet and the Dali lithographs lining the wall. "Inside the door, to the left, is a Biedermeier table. Remember it?"

"I saw a table with a black top and a regular wood-colored pillar holding it up. Two chairs."

"That's it. On the table was an oval tin with violets printed on it. About this big." She drew an oval on her palm.

"Nope," the detective said.

"No?" That couldn't be. She was sure the tin had been right there.

"Couple of cups and saucers, a fancy coffeepot, little spoons. That's it. No candy."

"But it was there. A new tin of them." She remembered Stroden's long fingers easing the container open and extracting the dusky pastille. "Wait—were the coffee dishes still out?"

"On the table. One of the coffee cups was, anyway. The other one fell to the floor."

"Mr. Stroden had offered me a pastille, but I didn't want it. He set it on my saucer. Check the floor. It's about the size of a navy bean." Someone had taken the tin. Her breathing quickened.

Roscoe took out his phone. Whoever he was calling answered immediately. "Are you still at the scene? Good. Check the dressing room carpet for a small candy. The witness says the victim ate one before he died."

Pepper emerged fully from under the chair and jumped into the detective's lap. Roscoe absently stroked him. Must have cats at home. "Says he doesn't see it."

"Keep looking," Joanna said. "If you decide his death was" –she fidgeted with the hem of her skirt—"murder, it had to be the pastille."

That night, when Joanna arrived home after closing Tallulah's Closet, her husband Paul was in the kitchen chopping vegetables, his German shepherd mix Gemma at his feet. Summer days were long, and warm light splashed over the counter. An old blues record was on the turntable— Robert Johnson, if Joanna wasn't mistaken. Living with Paul, she'd learned a lot about blues and jazz. In turn, Paul was developing a good touch for silk versus rayon versus cotton velvet, and once he'd even surprised her by bringing home the original and new versions of *Sabrina* to compare.

After the police interview, Joanna had returned to Tallulah's Closet. The customer with the garment bag had brought in seven delicate silk nightgowns, each cut on the bias and each a different pale pastel. They'd belonged to her mother, who'd worn a different nightgown every day of the week. The daughter had been unable to give them up until now, when she was moving into a condo and trimming her possessions.

Joanna had assured her that as hard as they were to give up, the nightgowns would create a lot of joy in the world. She'd carefully tied the sash of a watered daffodil-yellow gown. Chances were fifty-fifty it would be purchased as an evening gown rather than worn to bed. Either way, it was a beauty. The rest of the day was filled with the tasks of running a vintage clothing boutique: chatting with customers, emptying dressing rooms, sewing on buttons, dusting display cases.

Paul set down the knife and kissed her hello. "I put a cocktail glass in the freezer. Before he went out, Uncle Gene said you'd had a rough day."

"Did he give you details?"

"No. Said you'd better tell me. What happened?"

Joanna filled a cocktail shaker with ice and splashed gin over it before adding a touch of vermouth. Before she met Paul, she'd lived alone enough years to become used to dealing with her feelings on her own. It had taken months before she didn't assume Paul asked about her day simply out of courtesy. He really cared. Still, old habits died hard.

"Remember how I had an appointment to buy clothes this morning? You would have loved the trim in the entry hall, by the way. Walnut, I think." She wished the martini were already in her hand. "Anyway, the man who owned the house died while we were talking. At first, I thought it was a heart attack. Now, it looks like murder."

She wrapped the shaker in a dishtowel and shook it until ice slicked the shaker's wall. Gemma sat up. Paul raised an eyebrow and waited until the noise subsided before speaking.

"Murder? Jo!"

She pulled an etched cocktail glass from the freezer and poured the martini into it. "Lemon, please."

He held up a lemon. "Not until you tell me more."

As she recounted the events of the day, he handed her the lemon and a paring knife to make a twist. "So, the police are looking for the violet candy now. I bet you anything it's poisoned." She sipped the martini. Cold and citrusy. Delicious. "Plus, why would the whole tin disappear like that?" She set the glass on the counter and began to pace. "The question is, why? Why kill him, and why now?"

"You mentioned his memoir."

Joanna stabbed the air with a finger. "Exactly my first thought. Was he planning to spill the beans about something big?"

"People don't usually murder when you tell their secrets. They sue."

"Plus there's the question of how the murderer could have discovered that the story would be in the memoir to begin with. Stroden wouldn't tell me much about it."

Paul scraped diced vegetables and chicken into a bowl. He tossed a cube of roasted chicken to Gemma, who snapped it from the air. "You think someone's after his money?"

"He has a nice house. His furniture and art are probably worth a bundle, too. But, if so, why kill him now? Why not be patient and let time take care of it?" Joanna pulled plates from the cupboard and silverware from a drawer. "He did mention a movie that was filmed but never released. I asked him about it, but he implied it was too hot to get into, and that I'd have to wait until his memoir came out."

"An unreleased movie? Why kill for that?"

She set her unfinished martini next to her plate and poured a glass of water for Paul. He didn't drink. "I don't know. I don't get it. I almost saw some of its costumes. Edith Head designed them. He was two steps from opening the closet when he collapsed."

"Double tragedy this morning, then."

She bit off a laugh. "I knew you'd understand."

Paul set the chopped salad between them and sat. His voice was sober. "I haven't heard you this excited about something in months. Something tells me it's not just the movie costumes, either."

"Oh, you know." She avoided meeting his gaze and busied herself loading their plates. He'd hit on something. The murder investigation did fascinate her. "Bradley Stroden was no stranger to Gene—and his silver. Did I tell you that?"

"Uh oh."

"Sounds like he lifted some nice pieces of sterling. Probably paid for a few weeks of betting on the horses." She picked up her fork and set it down again without eating. "What are we going to do about him?"

Now neither of them was eating. Paul leaned back. "I don't know. Is he really bothering you?"

She looked at him—his jaw that always seemed to need shaving, the calluses on his hands, the strong arms. She loved him. Gene was his family. "No. It's just such a small house, that's all."

"You're right. I probably should talk to him about his plans. At least he's out most evenings."

The subject had safely switched from Stroden's murder to Gene. The tension in Joanna's shoulders released. "Have you ever wondered about that? About what he's doing?"

Paul pushed around some salad on his plate. "So, you've wondered, too? He swears he's not back in the business."

"Then who's he hanging out with? Something is going on. I wish I knew what. It wouldn't be good for any of us if he's tossed in prison again."

"He'd never get out, at his age." Paul sighed. Gemma echoed his sigh from beneath the table. "He's a good man, Jo. He truly is. After my dad died, he was it. I owe a lot to him."

"Sort of," she added. Gene had pressed Paul into lookout services once in a while and had given him a few lessons in the intricacies of alarm systems.

"True. He never got me into a situation where I was at risk, though."

"Because you were never caught," she reminded him.

"And when Kristin died"—Kristin, Paul's sister—"he was there for me, too."

"I know." She pulled his hand between hers and laced their fingers together. "I really do understand. He can stay as long as you want him here."

She released Paul's hand, and at last he dug into his dinner. Joanna ate, too, but her mind had drifted to Bradley Stroden again. What, exactly, had Stroden known that was so dangerous—if that's why he was killed? She saw him again on the floor, his mouth twisted and eyes screwed shut. Beyond him stretched the row of polished wardrobe doors.

"Don't worry about Uncle Gene. We'll figure it out," Paul said.

She leaned over and kissed his stubbly cheek. "I'm sure we will." But she was really thinking of how to get her hands on *Starlit Wonder*.

Chapter 4

The next morning, Joanna was at Portland's Central Library when its doors opened. A warm breeze rustled the leaves on the thick-trunked elms out front, casting a moving pattern of light on the sidewalk. Joanna waited on the steps while guards unlocked tall iron gates.

Inside, she climbed the curving marble staircase to the second floor, where the information desk shared a high-ceilinged room with the science collection and several rows of tables with computer terminals. The tables were beginning to fill with an odd combination of kids. Lots of them.

"Joanna, nice to see you." The pink-haired woman at the desk set down her coffee mug and smiled. With her full sleeves of tattoos and multiple piercings, she stood the cliché of "straight-laced librarian" on its head. "First customer of the day."

"Hi, Kelsey. I brought you a present." Joanna laid a pair of lemon yellow wrist-length dress gloves on the counter. "I thought you could wear them riding your bike. In the fall, before it gets too cold, but when you need a little something."

Kelsey beamed. "These are terrific. You wouldn't mind if I cut off the fingertips?"

"I was counting on it."

"Thank you." The librarian held the gloves at arm's length for a quick examination, then tucked them under the counter. "Now, how can I help you? Looking for a little more info on the relationship between Poiret and Schiaparelli? Or maybe you found a new costume jewelry mark?"

Joanna laughed. "No, none of that. I'm looking for an old movie script."

"Is it something obscure? We don't have a huge collection here, but I could probably order one through interlibrary loan."

"The film was called *Starlit Wonder*. It was made sometime in the mid-fifties but never released. I know it's a long shot, but could you check, anyway?"

"I'll take a look."

As the librarian clicked through screens on her computer, a few more teenagers filed in and slumped at tables. "Why so many kids today?" Joanna asked.

"It's the Story Challenge next week. We've been busy." Kelsey furrowed her brow. "I'm not finding anything so far."

"What's the Story Challenge?"

"A competition. The library hosts it every year during summer vacation. Middle schoolers across town read the same book, then they compete to answer questions about it. The winning team gets lunch with the governor." She pushed back from the computer. "I'm not finding the script. Are you sure you have the title right?"

"I think so. Would it help to know some of the cast? The wardrobe was by Edith Head, and one of the actresses was Kelly Rampton." Rampton's name had stuck in Joanna's mind, the only clue she had about the movie besides its name. "At least, I think that's it."

"No Kelly, but I do get a Callie. Could that be it? No listing of *Starlit Wonder* in the movie database, though."

"Try the script writer's personal papers," said a voice behind her.

She turned to find a freckled girl with sandy red hair and a serious expression. The girl quickly averted her eyes from Joanna's. Despite the late summer heat, she wore a light coat buttoned up to her neck. The coat was dusty beige with faux leather buttons and was probably sold with matching slacks — or maybe gauchos — at about the same time Tony Orlando and Dawn were on the radio's Top 40 playlist.

"That's a good idea," the librarian said. "You don't happen to know the writer's name, do you?"

"No, I don't. That's all I've got."

Kelsey dropped her hands from the keyboard. "I'm afraid I need more than this to go on. I'm sorry."

"Thanks, anyway. It was worth a try."

That was it, then. A dead end. It was probably for the best. Paul wouldn't want her getting involved, and Detective Roscoe didn't seem especially receptive, either.

To distract herself from her disappointment, Joanna turned to the redheaded girl. "That's a mid-1970s duster, isn't it? Maybe the JC Penney's house label?"

"I don't know," the girl said, once again avoiding her eyes.

"Stay-pressed twill really holds the heat. You must be warm."

Now the girl met her gaze. "I'm fine."

Joanna read the warning in her voice. "My name's Joanna. I own a vintage clothing store. That's why I asked about your coat."

The girl's expression relaxed. "I'm Mindy. How come you don't try to look up the script yourself?"

"I don't have a computer."

Joanna had spent her adult life watching as telephones went touch-tone, then became cordless, then ended up in purses with the ability to answer every question from John Wayne's birthdate to the name of the last ruler of the Ottoman Empire. People loved those phones. They viewed art exhibitions and mountain landscapes through its camera, communicated every few minutes with their thumbs, and couldn't find the optometrist's office without help from its GPS.

Joanna refused to give in. For one, she adored the slide of paper through her fingers and the weight of a telephone's handset. She saw no reason people couldn't wait a few hours to talk to her instead of expecting an instant reply text. And then there was the fact that older handbags were big enough only for a lipstick, sunglasses, and keys.

Giving technology the cold shoulder had its drawbacks, of course. One of them being the need to rely on the library's information desk. By now, she knew all the staff's clothing sizes and best colors.

Mindy squinted at her as if she'd emerged from *Starlit Wonder* herself. "You're joking."

"Not a bit."

"Not even a cell phone?"

"Nope. Mine has a dial and a cord attaching it to the wall."

"Hi, Mindy." Two girls slid into chairs across from Mindy. Although they greeted the redhead, they stared at Joanna.

"Hi. I'm Joanna. So, are you girls here for the competition, too?"

"Yeah," the girl with the black pixie cut said. Her fingernails were ragged and painted in peeling gold glitter. She pushed a non-existent hank of hair away from her eyes.

What an interesting group. Joanna shifted her examination to the third girl, who had thick eyelashes and a layer of baby fat that would likely burn off by high school. This girl dropped her gaze instantly. From the set of her lips, it was clear she didn't plan on talking.

"Do you have a name for your team?"

Joanna was beginning to feel some interest in the book competition. Maybe she didn't have a fancy phone, but she was a big reader. She glanced around the room. A posse of sharply groomed girls and boys, each of whom seemed to have either glasses or painfully white new tennis shoes, came into the room. Mindy and her friends were the underdogs. Not only was Joanna a reader, she was a fan of the underdog.

Mindy mumbled something Joanna couldn't quite make out.

"I'm sorry," Joanna said. "The what?"

"Book Bunnies," the brunette said. "We're the Book Bunnies."

A trim, tidy girl with a precise bob that probably echoed her mother's walked past the table. "Hello, *Book Bunnies*. I guess you'd better *hop* to studying if you want to beat us." The girl snickered.

Joanna watched the girl take a seat across the room. "Who was that comedic genius?"

"She's from another team. Athena's Warriors, they're called," Mindy said.

"Hmm. I'll be rooting for you," Joanna said. "Go, Book Bunnies."

Mindy smiled. When Joanna caught her eyes, she ducked her head and stared at the table. Joanna handed her a business card. "If you ever decide you want a new coat, come see me."

Mindy slipped the card into her pocket without looking either at her or the card.

Chapter 5

"Joanna? Where are you?" Paul yelled from the living room upstairs.

Joanna set down the kimono she was inspecting. "In the laundry room."

Their basement was divided into two sections. The first, at the bottom of the stairs, was a finished room remodeled sometime in the 1950s, with bead board paneling and a built-in bar. For now, this was where Gene slept. They'd moved the pink mid-century sectional sofa into Paul's shop in the garage, where it now did duty as the dog's hangout. In its place was a twin bed Gene had neatly made, pulling the sheets up as tightly as if he were a Marine. His clothing was precisely stacked in cupboards.

Through this room was the working part of the house — the furnace, laundry area, and storage. This evening Joanna sat with a stack of stained kimonos she'd bought at auction the week before, sorting the salvageable from the too-far-gone.

Paul's steps sounded on the stairs, Gemma at his heels. "Hi, Jo." He laid a copy of *The Oregonian* on her knees. "There's a piece in here about Bradley Stroden. In the obits. I marked the page."

"Thank you." She reached around his warm neck and breathed in the scent of wood and skin.

"Where's Uncle Gene?" he said.

"Don't know. He wasn't here when I got in."

"I'll make a plate for him anyway."

She opened the paper over the laundry sink while Paul returned upstairs. The sound of dresser drawers opening and the clunk of his work boots told her he was changing out of his work clothes.

Bradley Stroden's obituary was nearly a full column long. Besides what she already knew—his years with Edith Head, a short list of movies he'd helped on, and his time illustrating newspaper ads—she learned his studio had been upstairs in the old warehouse district now known as the Pearl District, and that he had breakfast most mornings at the counter at Fuller's Coffee House. It wasn't easy to reconcile his natty trousers and violet cologne with the fried eggs and working class banter at Fuller's.

Joanna leaned against the wall and folded down the paper to continue reading. Stroden's grandfather had had a business ferrying timber and other goods up the Willamette River. The obit dedicated a paragraph to the mansion itself, saying it had been built on the bluff to give Bradley's grandfather, Edwin Stroden, a prime spot in the tower for watching his ships. Edwin had fathered one child, a daughter, Bradley's mother, who died in 1958. Bradley was survived by a sister.

A memorial service was planned for next week. She read to the end, and then back again. The obituary didn't mention that Stroden had been murdered.

Slowly, she refolded the paper and set it aside. She picked up the nearest kimono and ran her fingers down its lining to check for fraying. Stroden's death was still ruled a homicide, wasn't it? Perhaps the newspaper hadn't caught on to it yet. Or the police had kept the information under wraps. She felt sure he'd been poisoned.

But, why? Who stood to gain from his death? Stroden lived in a huge house worth at least a few million dollars. Presumably, he owned it and it would go to the sister mentioned in the obituary. But why would a sister mail pastilles to her brother? She could slip the poison into a tin at any point and give it to him. It would be a lot less suspicious.

The memoir. Likely, most of the people he wrote about were well on in life, if not dead. He'd hinted at having some good stories, including some too hot to tell.

Which brought her back to *Starlit Wonder*.

Joanna pulled a pale green kimono with long sleeves from the pile. A dragon, embroidered in gold, crept around its hem. She lifted the garment by its shoulders. Yes, this one would command a good price. She knew at least three drag queens who would pull out their credit cards in a hot second. Her eyes lit on a tiny brown spot. She laid the kimono over her arm and examined it more closely. It looked like grease. A sprinkling of *terre de sommières* should take care of it. That is, if she could find the canister. A French customer had brought her the powder the spring before, saying it was ground to the texture of satin, and it worked miracles at absorbing oil. Joanna hadn't had the chance to use it yet.

She spread the kimono over her worktable and went to the shelf above the washing machine. Upstairs, the radio nattered the news while the sink ran off and on and the refrigerator and cupboard doors opened and shut.

The *terre de sommières* canister was wedged behind the jugs of white vinegar and bleach. She popped off its lid and tipped the container into her palm. Something lumpy tumbled from the powder. A chunk of earth?

No. She blew on the object and felt its edges. Metallic. She hurried it to the sink and rinsed the dust from its surface. She gasped as she turned the object in her fingers.

It was an emerald and diamond earring, and, if she wasn't mistaken, the real thing.

⁎⁎

Joanna took the earring to the light. She dusted it with an old washcloth, and grass-green light sparkled. Its fittings were platinum, she was pretty sure. The earring formed a cascading fan of diamonds with five teardrop-cut emeralds dangling below it. From the squared-off shape of the fittings, she judged it as Deco. The value of what she held in her palm could have paid off her house.

She clicked off the light and stared, slack-jawed. Where was the earring's mate? And why was it hiding in her stain remover? She closed her fingers around the earring. *Gene.*

"Jo, ready for dinner?" While she'd been absorbed in her find, Paul had come down the stairs. He put a hand on her shoulder. "What's wrong?"

"Look what I found." She opened her hand.

He took the earring from her, glanced at it, and handed it back. "Another orphan?"

Paul had picked up a few of her terms of art. "No. At least, not my orphan. I've never seen it before." She turned to him. "I think it's real. If it is, the stones alone are worth thousands. If it's Harry Winston or Cartier — and it could be either — it's worth a lot more than that."

They both looked through the doorway to Gene's room.

"You don't think—" Paul started.

"I don't know what to think."

Perhaps curious about their delay to the dinner table, Gemma joined them in the basement. Pepper wound around Joanna's feet.

"He has been gone a lot," Paul said.

"And he's so mysterious about it."

Paul shook his head. "No. No, I don't see it. He said he'd gone straight, and I believe him. I mean, if he were stealing again, why would he be living in our basement? He'd have rented an apartment where he could go about his business without us getting in the way. He'd have the money for it."

"Maybe we're his cover," she pointed out. "He can tell his parole officer he's working for you part time while he's really off breaking into houses."

"Where did you find it?"

"In a canister of stain remover at the back of the laundry shelf."

"The earring was in here?" He lifted the canister of *terre de sommières*. "Have you looked through the rest?"

"I hadn't gotten that far."

He set the newspaper on her worktable and tipped the canister's contents onto it. Another earring tumbled out. They stared at it. Paul drummed his fingers on the tabletop. "Come upstairs and eat. We can talk this through over dinner."

She held up the earrings. "What should we do with these?"

"Bring them both with you."

Upstairs, Paul had set the table with the wide faience soup bowls Joanna had found at an estate sale. A salad bowl sat between them. Joanna laid the earrings on the red-flowered tablecloth and polished them lightly with a cotton napkin. The gems glowed the color of a lawn at sunset.

Paul took a seat. "You think they're real, huh?"

"I'm almost sure of it." She tore her eyes away from the earrings and picked up the salad tongs. "What's for dinner?"

"One of the guys at the job site suggested this salad. It's chicken, peaches, tarragon, farro, scallions, and red bell pepper. Sounded odd, but he swore it was great."

Portland had to be one of the few places where construction workers talked gourmet food and listened to public radio as they worked. Once she'd met Paul at a foursquare he was helping to refurbish, and he asked her to pick up a six-pack of Pellegrino water on the way for the crew.

"It looks delicious. Thank you." She absently spooned some into her bowl. She began to unfold her napkin, then set it aside. "Do we say something to Gene about the earrings?"

"Do you know for sure they weren't in there before Gene moved in?"

"This was the first time I'd opened the canister." The dust on its cap and its position at the back of the laundry shelf were proof. They would also have tipped off Gene that it was a safe place to stash something. "But I'd have noticed if there was something clunky in it like this when I put it on the shelf. No, I'm sure they weren't in there."

"Then I guess we'll need to talk to him about it."

Joanna pushed a piece of chicken with her fork. "I'm sorry, Paul. Maybe there's an explanation." She knew they had the same thought. "I haven't seen anything in the news about a rash of high-end break-ins, have you? His crimes were a long time ago. Probably only the old-timers remember him, like Foster Crisp." Before Foster Crisp was in the homicide bureau, he'd worked larceny and played a long-running game of cat and mouse with Gene. "Plus, how likely is it that he'd simply steal one pair of earrings? Wouldn't he come home with more than that?"

"If he was working with a gang, someone else could have fenced the rest."

"But not the earrings?" On the street, a car door shutting drew Joanna's attention. The soprano murmur of a child's and woman's voices told her it wasn't Gene.

"I can't explain it. Maybe he's keeping them as a sort of savings account. Or maybe they're too recognizable to fence."

"Let's walk through what we know," Joanna said. "Gene has a history of robbery. He just got out of prison and is on parole."

"But he's clean now," Paul said. "He swears to it."

"I know, but hear me out. He doesn't seem to be in a hurry to find work. He disappears evenings and is cagey about where he's been." She caught his gaze. "I'm sorry, Paul. I'm just listing the facts."

He looked at his plate. "Go on."

"Someone—almost certainly him—hid a pair of emerald earrings somewhere a casual search would never find them. Chances are high they aren't Gene's earrings. He couldn't have inherited them from anyone in your family, could he?"

Paul snorted. "Not hardly."

She chose her next words carefully. "If he's in possession of jewelry that's not his, and he's found out, he's going back to prison." She drew a long breath. "And if the police learn we knew, and we'd done nothing about it, we could end up in the cell next to him."

A minute passed before Paul said, "I know."

"We could have the earrings appraised. A jeweler could tell us more about them. When they were made—they look Deco to me—what they're worth…"

"That's risky. I'm not sure what to do."

Could more stolen goods be hidden downstairs? She didn't want to raise this possibility and, frankly, didn't want to know. Neither did she want to be the person to question Gene. How would Paul handle this? They hadn't been together long enough that she could predict his reaction. To Joanna, the earrings were both of their problem, but Paul needed to take the lead on resolving it.

At last, she lifted a fork full of salad to her mouth. "This is good. Was it the sheetrocker who gave you the recipe? The same guy with the tip on biscuits?"

"Yep." He sighed. "I'll set some aside for Uncle Gene. And I'll talk to him." He slid a hand up her ring finger, bumping her wedding ring with his own. "We'll get to the bottom of this."

Chapter 6

The next morning, Joanna was at Tallulah's Closet, dusting the top of the jewelry display and pondering the fact that Gene hadn't returned last night, when Mindy entered the shop. Despite the threat of ninety-degree heat, the girl still wore the buttoned-up coat she had at the library. She stood, frozen, inside the door.

"It's so beautiful," Mindy finally said, her voice breathy.

"Come in. It's nice to see you."

Mindy's head turned as she took in the pastel fluff of organdie along the wall of party dresses and the sleek row of black cocktail dresses. A few inches of denim pant legs peeked from under the coat, but that was all Joanna saw.

"You must be roasting in that coat. Why don't you take it off?"

Her head snapped back to Joanna. "I'm fine."

Undeterred, Joanna pulled out a full-skirted sundress with a pattern of poodles across its bodice. "I bet you'd look great in this. Want to try it on?"

Mindy reverently touched the poplin skirt and inched closer. "Do you think it would fit?"

After eight years in the vintage clothing business, Joanna didn't need a tape measure to size up a customer. "Absolutely. It might be a bit long, but it would be a cinch to hem."

Mindy lifted the dress by the hanger and held it against her coat.

"The mirror's back there." Joanna pointed toward the rear of the store.

In a daze, Mindy walked toward the gold-framed mirror. Joanna saw a kid who knew how to shriek with laughter, but probably hadn't in a while. Mindy was intrigued, though. Joanna could tell. The girl's fingers rested on the coat's top buttons.

"Go ahead, try it on. You can lay your coat over that chair."

All at once, the girl's smile vanished and her hands dropped to her sides. "Thank you, but no." She returned the hanger to Joanna. "I need to go home. I just came because I heard you talking about an actress, Callie Rampton."

"Oh." Joanna was still puzzled.

"At the library. Remember? You asked about *Starlit Wonder* and mentioned Edith Head and Callie Rampton. I'm sorry to tell you that Edith Head died a long time ago."

"In 1981," Joanna said.

"Yeah. Way long ago."

"Practically when dinosaurs roamed the earth. What about Callie Rampton?"

"She's still alive. I found her address for you. You were interested, right? You said you don't use computers. So I looked it up. No big deal. You gave me your card." She handed Joanna a scrap of paper with Rampton's name, an address in Milwaukie—a suburb south of town—and Stamp Gurlz written on it. "Stamp Gurlz. That's her business."

"That's so thoughtful. And you have an amazing memory. Thank you."

The girl wasn't finished yet. She stood, absorbed in taking in the racks of frothy dresses. Her visit clearly wasn't about Callie Rampton's address alone.

"How are the rest of the Book Bunnies?" Joanna asked.

"Fine," she said in an emotionless voice.

"And that other team? The smarty pants team?"

"Athena's Warriors. They're fine, too. I guess."

"Well, I really appreciate your trouble with this. Will you let me give you something for your effort? Something small? Not clothes," Joanna added quickly, afraid she'd scare her off again.

Mindy's eyes darted toward the door, then back. "Something small?"

Joanna reached into the jewelry display case. "I was thinking of this charm bracelet." The bracelet, from the 1970s, had a chunky gold-tone chain and wasn't worth much, but she loved the tiny San Francisco street car and Leaning Tower of Pisa charms.

"Is that a cat on it?"

"With ruby eyes. Isn't it adorable?" Joanna laid the bracelet on the counter. "It's yours, if you want it. It's the least I can do for your trouble."

Mindy touched its clasp. "Yes, please. I mean, if it's okay."

"Want me to fasten it for you?"

"No. I can do it." She snatched the bracelet off the counter and clipped it around her tiny wrist. She tilted her hand side to side to watch the charms dangle. Her smile returned, bright and genuine. "Thank you."

"You're welcome."

Mindy waved and practically skipped to the door. "Bye."

"Come back soon," Joanna yelled to the khaki twill of her retreating back. What was that about? Mindy had gone to special effort, made a special trip.

Joanna relented and turned on the air conditioner. She preferred to stick to the fan, but it was too hot. Back at the tiki bar, she looked at the address again. Bradley Stroden had told her Callie Rampton had worked on the set of *Starlit Wonder*. Maybe she had a copy of the script—or could at least shed some light on the scandal behind the movie.

She'd call Detective Roscoe. He'd want this information. Maybe he already had it. In any case, it was the excuse she needed to dip her toes back into the investigation.

Joanna's call bounced into Detective Roscoe's voice mail. "I have a possible lead for you," she said. "Someone who knew Bradley Stroden. You have my phone number." She hung up feeling unconvinced she'd left a tantalizing enough message to merit a return call. The newspaper hadn't even mentioned that Stroden had been murdered. Could the police have dropped the case already?

It wasn't ten minutes later that Roscoe pushed open the door. He couldn't look more different than Mindy had earlier that morning. His hair puffed in frizz to rival Albert Einstein's. His tank-style T-shirt was clearly visible under the thin plaid of his button-down shirt.

"I'm glad you called," he said. "I was planning to get in touch with you, anyway."

"You were?" Joanna said. "Did you find out anything more?"

"Let's start with you. Why did you call?" He glanced over the store. "Anywhere to sit in this place?"

Unlike most visitors to Tallulah's Closet, Roscoe seemed unmoved by the shop's mélange of color and texture. Joanna pointed to the red bench at the room's center, and the detective positioned himself to take maximum advantage of the air conditioner.

Joanna leaned over the tiki bar. "When I was at Bradley Stroden's, he briefly mentioned an old colleague. I discovered she lives just south of town. I thought I'd pass along her name and address."

She copied the address from the paper Mindy had given her and pushed it across the bar. Roscoe looked at it but didn't rise to take it.

"Why is this name so helpful to me?"

"If she spent time with Stroden recently, she might have an idea if someone had threatened him, or if he'd been in some kind of trouble."

"Like maybe he knew someone with access to cyanide?"

Joanna pushed out from behind the bar and joined Roscoe on the bench. "Cyanide? Was that what was on the pastilles?"

"Let's back up a second. I want you to tell me about your visit to Stroden, starting from when you first saw him. Step by step."

"We already went through this. I won't have anything new to tell you—"

"Never mind that. Now, you first saw him downstairs, right?"

"Yes." She thought back to that morning, the sun washing the walnut trim with golden light, the roses and marigolds on the side table. "I was in what they called the 'morning room' at the far south side of the ground floor. Bradley Stroden came through the dining room—that's the room just off the foyer—"

Roscoe nodded. "Got it. Go on."

"Anyway, he hadn't quite got dressed yet. Despite the heat, he was wearing trousers"—meticulously pressed, she remembered—"and a smoking jacket, red brocade silk with chartreuse lining, also silk. The left sleeve had 'B. S.' embroidered on it in black. And glove leather slippers, probably Turkish."

The detective waved a hand. "We know what he was wearing. What else?"

"He invited me to come upstairs to see some clothing Edith Head had designed. He asked Luke to bring up coffee for two."

Roscoe held up a hand. "What did he say? Be as exact as you can."

"Let's see." She bit her lip and released it. "Luke asked if he was ready for his coffee, and he said to bring it to the dressing room and to include a cup for me."

"Did you see the coffee things?"

"Not then. Not until they came upstairs. Why? Do you think they were poisoned? You found the pastille, right?"

"Stroden's blood showed signs of cyanide poisoning, but we're not sure yet how it was ingested. The pastille's at the lab. But, go on. You said the coffee and cups were brought upstairs."

"Yes." Remembering, she could almost smell the heavy scent of coffee mixed with the violets that clung to the air. "I don't suppose you want a description of the coffee set?"

"Not necessary, thank you. Did he take sugar? Cream?"

Cyanide in the sugar bowl. Classic. "No. Just the pastille."

Roscoe nodded. "Okay, the pastilles. Were they on the tray?"

"Not on the tray. Luke brought them up."

"The secretary, huh?" He made a note.

"Yes. He said they'd come in the morning's mail, and Stroden mentioned they weren't his usual brand. I figured Mr. Stroden probably ordered them. Violet pastilles aren't easy to find in the United States. He opened a new package and offered me one—which I declined—before taking one himself. He set one on my saucer."

Roscoe put his hands on his knees and pushed himself up. "You're probably right. It was probably the pastille. You both drank the coffee.

We'll have the lab results back soon."

"Do you run into a lot of cyanide cases?" Joanna asked. "It sounds so — so old-fashioned."

"It is. Cyanide, arsenic, and strychnine used to be a wife's favorite way to become a widow, but you can't march down to the hardware store these days, complain about rats, and leave with a box of arsenic. Oh, we still see the odd canister of Cyanogus in the back of someone's garage, but most of the time the house's owner didn't even know it was there." He scratched his head, displacing a gray curl. "Well, until lately, that is. The Internet has made it easy again. No, most homicides these days are at the end of a gun."

"Somehow, old-fashioned seems right for him."

Roscoe fidgeted with his pen and stared beyond Joanna. "If the candy tests positive for cyanide, Stroden's death was premeditated, no two ways about it."

"He told me he had a habit of eating pastilles. Had for years. Said he always had a tin."

"Somebody else knew it, too." He pulled keys from his front pants pocket. "Lucky they're not a habit for you."

"Have you figured out why someone would kill him?" Joanna nodded toward one end of the red bench, hoping Roscoe would follow her lead and sit again. After hesitating, he did.

"That's not the approach I take. Motive is too far ranging to consider right away. People kill because of anything from a knee-jerk reaction to an insult to a long-planned strategy to get the family jewels."

Thinking of Uncle Gene, Joanna winced.

"First, I examine means and opportunity," Roscoe said. "Who could have had the means—"

"In this case, poison."

"Right. And who could have administered it."

"Motive matters, though," Joanna said. "If you isolate why a person was killed, can't it help limit the pool of suspects? For instance, Stroden was writing a memoir."

"You brought that up before, and we'll certainly examine it. But, look. Chances are that most of the people he wrote about are dead. His memoir might make good reading, but it's old news. Money is probably a better motive."

"So, he's rich?" Joanna asked. "He lives like it."

"We're not there yet. Like I said, right now we're focusing on means and opportunity." Again, he heaved himself to standing. "There's one more thing."

"What is it?"

"Your name came up a few times in our homicide records."

"That was just by chance," Joanna said. "I just happened—"

Roscoe put up a palm. "I know, I know. You weren't convicted of anything. But you insinuated yourself into a couple of investigations. I appreciate you giving me Rampton's name and address, but we already have it. That's what we do. Getting involved in a homicide case is a sure way to sour our work and put your own safety at risk. Got it?"

Joanna stared at him without responding. He was telling her to back off. Her pulse remained even, but defiance rippled through her bloodstream. How dare he condescend to her? The police might have labs and computers on their side, but she was observant. She had a knack for the telling detail. If she hadn't asked a few questions over the past couple of years, the police's cold case files would be a lot fatter.

"Understand?" he repeated. "Crisp was more patient than I am."

"I understand all right." She fastened him with her gaze. "Definitely."

"You promise you'll back off?"

She widened her lips in a smile she was afraid looked more like a grimace. "What would be my motive for getting involved?"

"You have the means and the opportunity. That's enough for me."

Chapter 1

Callie Rampton's hobby shop occupied the front of a modest white bungalow at the edge of Milwaukie's downtown. Many Portlanders ignored the suburb directly to its south, not out of snobbery, but simply because they forgot about it. To them, Milwaukie signaled grandma-like houses festooned with petunias, and a high school turning out classes of insurance agents and dental assistants.

Until now, Joanna's sole exposure to Milwaukie had taken place in a church parking lot. A woman had called Tallulah's Closet saying she had an old suit of her mother's, and if Joanna wanted it, she'd better come and get it. Joanna had had to resist gasping with joy when she saw the suit. It was by Fred A. Block, and brass studs ornamented the jacket, from the broad 1940s-style shoulders to its narrow waist. It was in mint condition and begged for seamed stockings and a veiled hat.

After granting Joanna a thirty-second peek, the woman had zipped the wardrobe bag closed. "I won't take less than fifty dollars," she'd demanded.

Joanna had handed her the cash with one hand and taken the suit with the other. Fred A. Block was a collector's dream label, and his suits were nearly impossible to find. Within the week, she'd sold it for nine hundred dollars.

After a few wrong turns, Joanna at last pulled into the hobby shop's driveway. The sign propped in what used to be the living room's front window said, "Open."

"Welcome to Stamp Gurlz." An older woman cut on the lines of a zaftig Marilyn Monroe stood behind the counter with a pair of scissors in her hands. She wore stark black glasses with circular lenses. "May I help you?"

Shelves stuffed with rubber stamps lined the room. The stamps bore patterns of everything from kittens and roadsters to high-heeled shoes and even a vintage girdle. A table on one side held a rainbow of inkpads. On the back counter, a television played on mute.

"I'm looking for Callie Rampton."

"Not rubber stamps?"

"No. Although they're lovely." She stepped forward. "I have a shop, too, but I sell vintage clothing."

"Retail's tough. Thank goodness for the Internet, or I'd have been out of business a long time ago. Those Nebraskan ladies like their rubber stamps."

The woman's voice had warmed. Joanna relaxed a bit. "I still haven't ventured online for sales. I should, though."

The woman set down her scissors and gave Joanna a once-over. "I'm Callie. Autograph hunter? I bet you're a film buff."

"No. That is, I do like old movies, and Bradley Stroden told me you're an actress. But I'm not here about that. I'm here about Mr. Stroden, actually."

"No kidding. Poor man. I had to read his obit three times over. I just couldn't believe it." Callie Rampton came around the counter. "Pleased to meet you."

"Joanna Hayworth."

The older woman's grip was warm and friendly. "Have a seat, there on the sofa."

In the room's corner, partially hidden by the counter but with a view of the door, were two sections of an old ivory sectional sofa with silver thread running through the upholstery. They faced each other over a narrow coffee table piled with craft magazines.

"I love your glasses. Edith Head had glasses like that, didn't she?" Joanna said.

"Had several pairs. In fact, this is one of them. I begged her for them before I left Hollywood, and she gave me one of her old pairs."

"No kidding." The same glasses that had sat on Edith Head's nose. Joanna longed to touch them.

"You want to try them on, don't you?"

"Oh, I wouldn't dare ask—"

"Here." Callie slipped them off her face. "Everyone does. Go ahead and put them on."

Slowly, Joanna ran a finger over the frame's curves. She lifted the flap on her purse. "Let me find my compact. I've got to see this."

"I'd give you a mirror, but you're not going to be able to make anything out."

Open compact in hand, Joanna slid the glasses over her ears. She opened her eyes to look through the same frames Head might have looked through when she designed the costumes for *To Catch a Thief*. Callie was right, though. Her reflection was a blur. Joanna looked around the room. She could tell it was daylight, but that was about all. The couch's fuzzy blob of ivory came into focus as she took off the glasses.

"Told you. Two astigmatisms and a strong prescription will do that." Callie nudged the glasses up her nose with the back of a knuckle. "I haven't heard Bradley mention you. Are you one of his friends from Fuller's?"

"The diner? No, I'm afraid I was with Mr. Stroden when he collapsed. The police think it was murder."

"Murder!" Callie gasped. "Are you sure? I didn't see it in the papers."

Joanna nodded. "I'm sorry to tell you this way. I'm sure the news will come out soon."

"Murder," she repeated. "Who would kill Bradley?"

"The police don't know yet."

"I have a good security system and a Smith and Wesson back-up, but you can't be too careful." Once again, Rampton looked her over, pausing to examine Joanna's stack of Bakelite bangles. "Why are you here, anyway? Not just to tell me how Bradley died?"

"I feel"—Joanna pondered a moment—"responsible." And curious. "He was working on his memoir when he died. I wondered if he might have been sitting on stories people didn't want to get out. I thought you might have an idea."

"I knew Bradley, you're right. We worked together, oh, jeez, at least sixty years ago."

Which put Rampton in her late seventies or early eighties. She was no blue-haired granny, but platinum-haired. With red lips and a best-friend smile in the Joan Blondell mold.

"With Edith Head," Joanna said.

"Oh, Edie never dressed me. She stuck with the stars. No, her assistants dealt with the riffraff like me." She absently stacked a few magazines, lining up their edges. "Murder, huh? You think he was killed for something he knew? Bradley got around, it's true, but he never blabbed."

"I spent only half an hour with him. But he did mention one

situation in particular. It's where your name came up." She looked Rampton in the eyes. "*Starlit Wonder*."

The actress's face froze before melting into a cheerful smile. As she opened her mouth to speak, her cell phone rang from across the room. She rose to look at its screen, tapped it once, and set it down. "*Starlit Wonder*," Rampton repeated. Her gaze sharpened. "You're in the vintage clothing business, huh?"

"Yes. That's why I was at his house. Mr. Stroden had some dresses to sell."

"Do you use rubber stamps?"

"No." Somehow the conversation had gone off track. "But Stroden—"

"Rubber stamps could really enhance your brand, you know." Callie rose from the couch and went to a nearby shelf. "Take this one, for instance. It's from an old Japanese dressmaker's manual."

The stamp showed a woman's torso with gridlines indicating where to measure. "That's nice, but—"

"You could use it to stamp bags or notes. This one would be good, too. And this."

Joanna turned two more stamps in her hand. One showed a woman's curler-topped head. The other was of a round-toed 1930s pump. "These are great."

"I could customize a stamp for you, too. Maybe something with the name of your shop."

Joanna set the stamps firmly on the table. "Getting back to *Starlit Wonder*. Can you think of any reason the film would be scandalous?"

Callie avoided her gaze. "I only played a minor role. The heroine's best friend."

"Why wasn't the film ever released?"

"Could have been for lots of reasons. It happened sometimes. It was a long time ago."

This time Joanna kept her mouth shut and stared. Callie would be forced to speak eventually.

"Okay, the producer was a bit of a horndog."

"What?"

Callie sighed. "You asked about controversy. The producer—David Sipriano was his name, we called him Big Sip—hit on all the girls. We just shrugged it off."

"That couldn't have been easy. It could cost you roles, right?" The Hollywood casting couch was legendary.

"Not so much that. The directors were worse, and, really, Sip was a good guy. No, we were all afraid of his wife. She caught one girl I knew." Callie turned toward the window. Sun illuminated the laugh lines around her eyes. "Sip and the girl took the ferry to Catalina for the day, and somehow Sip's wife got wind of it. She chartered a boat and nearly drowned the poor girl. Spent the rest of her career painting sets." Callie returned her gaze to Joanna. "Sip was terrified his wife would find out about his dalliances, and so were we. His wife had been an actress, too, back in the day. She knew her husband's predilections."

"Is that something this producer would be desperate to protect? I mean, if Bradley Stroden was planning to reveal it in his memoir?"

"No. I don't see it. It was so long ago, and it was public knowledge." She shook her head to emphasize the point. "No." Callie reached to her side and pulled down a rubber stamp of a snap-top alligator bag. "You might want this one, too."

"Why would a producer's affairs lead to a movie being pulled?"

Callie shrugged. "Don't know. You asked if there was any

controversy about *Starlit Wonder*, and that's all I could think of."
She set the stamp with the rest of the pile near Joanna.

Callie's tone made it clear she was finished with this line of questioning, but Joanna pressed on. Heck, she'd driven all the way out here, and she wasn't going home with a nine-hundred-dollar suit this time. "Did you see Mr. Stroden much over the years?"

"Bradley? Oh, sure. A few of us get together from time to time to talk about the old days. We go to the bar at the Benson Hotel or to Fuller's. Not as often as we used to, and, of course, there are fewer of us now." Her smile dimmed. "I'll miss him. Bradley. Murder. I still can't believe it."

Joanna pictured the potted palms in the old hotel's lobby and the leather-padded benches lining the bar. "That sounds nice. I didn't know that many Hollywood types had settled here."

"There are a few of us, besides Bradley and his sister."

"I read about the sister in the obituary, but I didn't know she lived in town."

"Sure. She used to be in Hollywood, too. An actress. Went by the name of Margay. You didn't meet her at Bradley's?" Callie started bundling the rubber stamps she'd set aside for Joanna as if the sale were a done deal.

Joanna shook her head. "Just his secretary and his housekeeper."

"Did the housekeeper have long white hair in ringlets?"

She nodded.

"That was Mary Pat. Margay. She's his sister."

Chapter 8

Joanna deposited her bag of new rubber stamps on the tiki bar at Tallulah's Closet and hauled the sandwich board to the sidewalk to announce that the shop was open for business. The sun on the awning told her that the day was going to be a scorcher.

She didn't know if her visit with Callie Rampton had been a success or not. Callie seemed to be holding out, but about what, Joanna couldn't say.

A crowd of brunch-goers stood outside the hip cafe facing the shop, many of them holding mugs of coffee and checking their names against the list at the door. Why people would wait an hour on the sidewalk for breakfast was beyond Joanna, especially when a perfectly good diner with no line at all was a ten-minute walk away. Sure, the video poker machines beeped from the bar, and the crusty owner was likely to stop by your table and chat while your omelet cooled, but the pancakes were terrific. One benefit of the busy restaurant, though, was the number of customers it drew to Tallulah's Closet.

She put the day's first record on the turntable. Early Sonny and Cher. "The Beat Goes On" was just what she needed. Joanna smiled at a customer who'd wandered over from the cafe across the street with a greasy box of leftovers and set it on a stack of freshly laundered handkerchiefs.

"Finding everything you need?" Joanna lifted the box. "I'll keep this for you at the counter."

When the customer turned for the door, having bought nothing, and returning only when Joanna reminded her that her leftovers were still on the counter, Joanna picked up the phone. Task number one, see Callie Rampton. Check. Number two, call Foster Crisp.

When Joanna had seen him last, Crisp hadn't yet retired from his position as a homicide detective with the Portland Police Bureau. Despite their sometimes-troubled relationship, Joanna liked to think Crisp had developed a begrudging respect for her. Maybe even a liking. She certainly liked and respected him — and feared him sometimes. He had a way of looking at her that made her sure he'd suss out every white lie. When he'd retired, Crisp had given her his cell phone number and suggested they keep in touch.

That was last spring. She hadn't even looked at his number since then. She hadn't needed to. Now Gene had been gone for two days, and they were sitting on a pasha's ransom of diamonds and emeralds.

He picked up the call on the first ring.

"Detective Crisp?" Joanna realized she'd never called him by anything but his title. "It's Joanna Hayworth."

"No 'detective' anymore. How about plain old Foster?"

"Foster," she said. It felt too familiar, but it was better than Mr. Crisp.

"I heard you were on the spot when Bradley Stroden was murdered."

"Word gets out fast," Joanna said. "Is the murder public yet?"

"I keep in touch with the department. Sounds like they're making a public statement today. The press release might have already gone out. What can I do for you? It doesn't have to do with the Stroden case, does it?"

"No. Not yet, anyway," she amended. "Remember Paul's uncle, Gene?" She knew he remembered. He'd made a point of mentioning Gene's livelihood when he first ran into Paul at Tallulah's Closet almost two years ago. His narrowed gaze at Paul had told her he knew something about Paul's unwitting involvement in it, too.

After small talk about Joanna and Paul's wedding and Crisp's retirement, he brought the conversation around to Gene again. "On parole, isn't he?"

Joanna hesitated. "You're a private citizen now, right?"

He didn't miss a beat. "Joanna, I have a responsibility to report anything you tell me about something illegal."

"Oh." The heat was rising. She clicked on the tiki bar's counter fan.

"Of course, if it's something you don't know for sure is illegal, or, say, you had a theoretical question about someone you know, I might be able to weigh in on that."

One hand fidgeted with the phone cord. "It's like this. I know someone who used to be a thief, but isn't anymore."

"Are you sure about that?"

No comment, she thought. "Yes," she said.

"But what?"

"But someone I know may have found a pair of valuable earrings in her house."

"And the ex-thief was in the house, too?"

"Possibly."

"The earrings might legally belong to the thief. There's no law against owning earrings."

Uncle Gene in emerald chandeliers? Unlikely. But she understood where this train of thought was headed. "Is there a registry for stolen jewelry?"

"No. Art and guns, yes. But jewelry? No."

Crisp was no longer a policeman. She couldn't trust a cop with information that might violate Gene's parole. Although that would be one way of getting him out of the basement, she noted wryly. She was already in dangerous waters. Paul didn't know she was having this conversation.

"I don't suppose you have any way to track down stolen jewelry anymore?"

"No. But I've been…"

It wasn't like Crisp to let his thoughts wander off without tying them up. "Been what?"

"Shoot. I've been bored. I still have a lot of good years left in me. My wife is ready to send me on a long cruise. By myself."

"Strangely, I understand." She'd been involved in a few crime cases, and they'd been enough to whet her appetite for the mental puzzles and surges of adrenaline.

"Paul's ready to get rid of you?"

"No, not that. But I understand how you'd miss your work. It's so interesting. Exciting, too. You never know what you're going to find. It would be hard to give up the challenge."

He made a noise that was a cross between a sigh and a groan. "I feel like a horse trained to work the fields, and now I'm back in the stable. I'm antsy."

"Does that mean you're thinking of going back to work? Or maybe buying a ranch?" Crisp had been raised in rural Eastern Oregon, and still sported cowboy boots and talked longingly of Ponderosa pines.

"No. Maybe someday, but not right now. No, I'm ramping up to hang out my shingle as a private investigator. The only thing is that I don't have any clients. Unless that's what you're calling about."

Joanna held up her hand to the fan's breeze. Ignoring her pounding heart, she asked, "How much would it cost to see if a particular item was stolen? If I were your client, that is?"

"Why don't we start at the beginning, Joanna? Tell me about this item. You might need to send me a photo — or have someone help you with that." He knew her limitations with technology.

She didn't need a photograph for a precise description. "It's a pair of diamond and emerald earrings, probably from the 1920s. Each earring dangles from a post in a fan shape. The body of the fan is figured in diamonds. Dangling from the bottom of the fan are teardrop-shaped emeralds. I'm not sure about total karats, but—"

"Platinum setting?"

"Yes." She raised an eyebrow.

"I don't need a database to tell me about those earrings. They're stolen, all right."

Joanna's heart sank. "Are you sure? You haven't even seen them."

"About two inches long?"

"Yes," she said reluctantly.

"Definitely stolen. It was a huge case. You didn't happen to find a matching necklace and brooch, did you?"

"Just earrings." Although who knew what would turn up in a thorough search?

"You're sure? The necklace was spectacular. Half a diamond mine must have been looted for it. The insurance settlement was stupendous."

"Oh. I'm surprised I didn't read about it." Joanna barely heard the words she spoke. Stolen. Paul would be devastated.

"I'd be surprised if you did. They were boosted more than forty years ago."

Chapter 5

"Forty years?" Joanna tightened her grip on the phone. "Did I hear you right?"

"Forty-four years, to be precise. It was a big deal," Foster Crisp said. "The crime was never solved. I had a photo of the stolen jewelry hanging over my desk until I left for Homicide. We used to joke that whoever solved the case would get two weeks of vacation and a spiral-cut ham."

The early 1970s. Gene might have been involved in the original job. Then why didn't he sell them? Or maybe he had stolen them from the jewelry's original thief?

"Tell me more about the case."

"June and I had just gotten married and were taking off for our honeymoon when the call came in." He cleared his throat. "We never did get that honeymoon."

"It was that important a case?"

"The jewelry—like I said, a full set—was originally from an old French count's family. They were so famous they had a name, the Greffulhe jewels. They belonged to a woman associated with the Canadian ambassador."

Joanna's thoughts shot back to her home, secured only by an elderly mutt and a single bolt deadlock. "No kidding."

"It gets worse. They were stolen from Senator Woodstock's house. The Canadian ambassador was visiting, and Woodstock had put him up. He was here on some sort of trade deal with lumber and salmon. That part wasn't important. The big deal was the pressure the governor put on the mayor and the mayor passed down to the chief to solve the case."

"No wonder you remember it."

"Oh, yes. After a beer, we old-timers still chat about it."

"You say the theft happened here in Portland?

"Woodstock had a guest suite in the coach house behind his house in the West Hills. That's where the ambassador stayed. It was a pretty slick crime. Not only did Woodstock have the U.S. Protective Service on duty, the ambassador had his own security. All the evidence pointed to one particular crew."

Joanna knew what was coming next. "You mean Gene, of course."

"Always at the top of our list at the time. Thing is, he couldn't have made the heist. He was in Idaho."

"Idaho?" It hardly seemed like the first place Gene would vacation.

"Near Coeur d'Alene. Said he was fishing, if I remember right. His alibi checked out. The chief lost his job the next year, and rumor had it it was because of Woodstock."

"So the jewels belonged to the ambassador's wife?"

"Nope. His mistress. That made the case doubly difficult. Word couldn't get out that there was a case at all." Crisp had a new energy in his voice. Joanna imagined him sitting straighter now with a hint of a smile on his lips.

She sat in silence, letting Crisp's story sink in. "Wow."

"Now if you have those jewels…"

"I'm not sure," Joanna said. "I might be mistaken. It was probably just a piece of costume junk that got lost in the laundry."

A long moment passed before Crisp replied. "I know you want to protect Gene, but don't make any fatal mistakes, Joanna. It's not just Gene's future you're talking about."

Now it was her turn to pause. "I'll be in touch. I just—I just need a bit of time. That's all."

"Then I'll be waiting to hear from you."

The next morning, Joanna cut her engine in the cul-de-sac below the Stroden mansion. Memories of the same place, same time a few days earlier washed over her. She hesitated before opening the car door.

After her call last night, Stroden's secretary, Luke, had been will-ing—even eager—to see her. She had started to roll out her excuse for wanting to drop by again, but he'd cut in, saying, "Does ten o'clock work?" It had been easy. Maybe too easy.

Today was Apple's day at Tallulah's Closet, so ten o'clock was per-fect, but that's about all that was going right. She still hadn't figured out how to tell Paul about the Greffulhe jewels, because it would mean letting on that she'd spilled the whole story to Crisp without talking it over first. It had felt so natural to pick up the phone to call Crisp. She had only been trying to help. Coloring her indignation at having to report every move—okay, maybe not every move—was the knowledge that her actions affected both of them. The better part of her urged her to tell Paul, and she would. Later.

As a result, breakfast had been uncomfortably silent. Gene had still not returned.

Now at the Stroden home, she leaned against her car and looked around. The last time she'd come, she was so excited to get into the butter-yellow mansion she'd wondered about for so long that she'd leapt up the steps. Today, she took a moment to look around.

At some point over the years, the house's grounds had been sold off. Rundown apartment complexes boxed it in. Here, the stream of ant-like traffic just over the embankment that had looked so charming from the morning room's windows was an exhaust-heavy roar of commuters. The mansion was a prim lady with thugs squatting around her.

Joanna started up the long flight of cement stairs. As happened the last time, the neighbor's curtains ruffled. Joanna smiled and waved. *Take that.*

Luke answered the door. The entry hall still shone with wood polish, but instead of violets, a Chinese urn full of dinner plate dahlias splashed pink and purple from the table just inside the door. Above them hung a gilded portrait of a meaty woman in a cloche scowling and clutching a lap dog. She made Auntie V look like Glinda the Good Witch.

"Like it?" Luke said, nodding at the portrait.

"The dog's cute," Joanna replied.

"That's Heidi, a toy fox terrier. According to Bradley, she was a real princess. But, yeah, she's pretty cute. The other one's Stroden *mère*. She doesn't come off very flattering in the memoir." He turned his back to the painting. "Take a right this time. We'll go to the parlor."

Luke led her to a room on the opposite side of the hall from her first visit. They were in a formal salon with a mix of Victorian and brightly colored Memphis furniture, as if the Queen Mother had wandered into Studio 54. Through an arch, she made out yet another room, this one lined in bookcases.

"I'm glad you're still interested in Mr. Stroden's clothing. I wouldn't blame you if you never wanted to come this way again."

"It was horrible, I admit. Murder." She shook her head. "But it was worse for you and Mr. Stroden's sister." She met Luke's eyes to confirm that the woman she'd met was, in fact, Stroden's sister.

"Mary Pat," he said. "She's not taking it well. She's at the doctor's office right now, in fact. I hope he gives her something to relax her. But enough of that. You're here for the clothes."

Truth was, she barely remembered the racks of clothing from that morning. She wanted to lead conversation to Stroden's memoir. Stroden had dictated it to Luke. If anyone knew if there was something incriminating in it, including about *Starlit Wonder*, it would be his secretary. And, of course, the possibility of getting her hands on the Edith Head wardrobe hadn't escaped her, either.

"We could go through the clothing, mark what you're interested in, then I'll let Mary Pat know. She inherits all this, of course."

"Sounds good." She took in the furniture, the rugs, the 19th-century landscape over the fireplace. "At least she won't have to worry about finances."

He shrugged. "She'll have to sell, which is why I'm sure she'll be glad to see Mr. Stroden's collection go to a good home."

"Have to sell?"

"Sure. The place is mortgaged to here." He chopped a hand to his neck. "Let's look at the clothes again."

Debt was a strong motivation for blackmail. Then again, a blackmailer—unless he was bad at his business—wouldn't be broke. They climbed the stairs to the landing with its row of Dali lithographs, walked by the room Joanna had entered with Stroden, and arrived at Stroden's bedroom.

Luke pulled back curtains on a bank of windows. This bedroom must have been Stroden's grandfather's at one time. It was large enough for an armchair, a desk, a fireplace, and a four-poster mahogany bed neatly made with three rows of pillows. A converted gas light fixture with frosted globes hung from the ceiling. Behind Joanna was the door to the dressing room where Stroden had died.

"Do you live here, too?"

"Down the hall. Although I don't know how much longer that will be."

"I'm sorry. This has to be rough on you."

"I'll get by." Luke pointed toward the clothing rack. "Anyway, there it is."

Joanna set her purse in the nearby armchair. "Should I just put to one side of the rack the things I'm interested in?" The key would be to get him talking about Stroden. See if anything in particular jumped out in the memoir. See if anything was worth killing for.

"Sure. Just hang them on this side of the rack."

Joanna flipped through the garments. If she were at an estate sale, a bare five minutes would be enough for her to assess them and make a decision. She wanted more than five minutes, so she slowed her hand. "I suppose the police must have questioned you?"

"Definitely. It's not over yet, either."

"That's too bad." She pulled an Italian wool jersey jacket from the rack. They were good between-weather wear in Portland, and the boxy cut suited every woman except the bustiest. "Detective Roscoe paid me a visit, too."

Luke sat at the edge of the desk. "Really? What did he want to know?"

"Probably the same things he asked you. Where I was, what happened. To tell the truth, I was surprised to see the police. I'd thought Mr. Stroden had a heart attack or something." She glanced at Luke from the corner of her eyes. His jaw muscles tightened.

"You saw the paper this morning?" he asked. "They're saying it was murder."

"I got that idea from Roscoe. He was especially interested in the violet pastilles." Luke didn't need to know she'd given the police that lead. "What else did they ask?"

"They wanted to know if anyone had threatened him, of course. I open his mail and screen his email—he never really took to his computer—but as far as I know, he didn't have any enemies."

"I imagine they wanted to talk about his memoir," Joanna said. She added two late 1950s silk blouses to the pile. As gorgeously tailored as they were, they weren't big sellers. Not many of her customers wore suits.

"Not much. No one really knew he was writing a memoir, anyway. So, who would threaten him?"

Joanna turned toward Luke. "You mentioned that the house is mortgaged. Did it ever cross your mind he might have blackmailed someone? You know, threatened to write about them in his memoir unless they paid up?"

She hadn't known how Luke would take this statement. Maybe he'd fly into a rage and throw her out. Maybe he'd be unmoved. Surely the police had gone down this path.

Luke's face reddened. "Blackmail?" he stammered. "I don't think so. That's not like him at all."

"He needed the money. You said so, yourself."

He took a moment uncrossing his arms and stretching his

shoulders. When he faced Joanna again, it was with more composure. "Remember, I opened all his mail." He began to shake his head, then stopped, as if remembering something.

"You know what's in his memoir. You would know if Mr. Stroden was planning to tell stories that certain people wouldn't want revealed."

"He wasn't cruel, you know. Or stupid. I'm sure he would have gotten in touch with anyone he planned to write about."

"You would have written those letters, right? So, you'd know."

"Look. I don't know anything, all right? I didn't keep track of everything he did. I just took dictation and cleaned up his grammar. Anyway, I don't see why it matters to you."

Joanna waited for more, but he didn't go on. "I see." She pulled a pair of white wrist gloves from a box and added them to the pile. Sadly, they weren't big sellers, either, as much as she loved them. People now counted on chemical peels to de-freckle their hands, not a preventative layer of cotton. "I'd love to buy these things," she said, pointing to the clothing she'd set aside. "If Mr. Stroden's sister agrees."

"I'll talk to her about it. I don't know why she wouldn't be happy to make some money from this. Especially given…"

"Yes."

The clock on the mantel above the fireplace seemed to tick especially loudly.

"There's just one thing," Joanna said. She turned toward the dressing room and stared at the closed door.

"Yes?" Luke was standing now, still crossing his arms.

"The wardrobe from *Starlit Wonder*."

"The Edith Head wardrobe."

"Do you think I could see it? I might be able to sell it for you."

Luke dropped his arms. "*Starlit Wonder*."

"That's right." She looked him in the eyes. "Mr. Stroden said there was quite a story around that film. He specifically mentioned it."

"The memoir does discuss *Starlit Wonder*."

"What was the film about, anyway?"

Luke's smile faltered. "What does it matter now?" When she didn't respond, he added, "It's not up to me to talk about what he wrote. I'm sure you understand."

"Of course." Joanna counted one, two, then three breaths.

"I think I can find the key to those wardrobes," he said at last.

He'd neatly avoided talking about the memoir, but the prospect of seeing Edith Head's work—work that hadn't received public recognition—made it easier for her to set that aside for the moment.

"I have contacts at a few major museums," she said. "Maybe I could help arrange a sale. Head is such a legend. She's overdue for an exhibition." Even a modest commission would be helpful to Joanna's bottom line. Plus, she'd get to examine the costumes inside and out.

Luke went to the mahogany desk with its green leather inlay that looked as if it had never been used. He drew keys from his pocket and opened a lower desk drawer, then took another key ring from that drawer.

"I think this is it. Let's try."

She fought to steady her breath as she followed him to the dressing room where she'd sat with Stroden only a few days ago. Violet perfume still clung to the air, but faintly enough that she might have imagined it. The table had been set upright, and the pastilles were long gone. But the rows of polished wardrobe doors remained, beckoning.

"This should be the key. Let's see if it works." Luke attempted to insert a brass skeleton key into a keyhole, but it didn't fit. "Maybe this one." He tried the key next to it, another skeleton key, this one polished to a golden sheen. It slid in on the first try. Before he could pull open the door, a voice yelled from the hall.

"Stop!" It was Stroden's sister, Mary Pat. She stood trembling outside the dressing room door. Her cheeks burned red, and her mouth was taut. "You." She seemed to have difficulty spitting out the words. "You killed him."

"What? I tried to save his life."

A drop of spittle stuck to her jaw. "He was alive until you came. Now they say he was poisoned."

Joanna grasped the back of a chair to steady herself. "No. Not at all, I mean, yes, he was killed, but—"

"Get out. Get out of this house."

"I don't know what you think, but it's not that. Please—"

"I said, get out. Now."

The words rang in Joanna's ears as she hurried down the stairs and into the street.

Chapter 10

As Joanna went through the rest of the day—stopping by the dry cleaners for a Ceil Chapman gown that needed special attention for its delicate beading; taking Pepper to the vet for vaccinations; checking out a thrift store that often had vintage Mexican purses in stock—Mary Pat's words rang through her head.

He was alive until you came.

Did she really think so, or was it grief? She should have known better than to show up at the mansion empty-handed. She could have brought flowers and a card. Anything. Instead, when Stroden's sister had arrived home, she'd found Joanna rifling through her brother's things.

"You killed it," the thrift store cashier said. Joanna started. "I think you got the best stuff in the store. Did you see the hot pink Bruno Magli pumps?"

Heart rate calming, Joanna said, "I did. They're fabulous, but they're only a size six." Sizes seven to nine flew out of the store, leaving her with a growing collection of shoes for doll-sized feet.

She gathered up her packages and drove home. Paul should still be at work, and Gene had been gone three days now. She checked for him every morning and night, and knew he'd be home eventually, as long as the earrings were still here. In the meantime, home had been peaceful, almost like the old days.

She wistfully remembered back only a few years ago when she was single and could take uninterrupted naps whenever she wanted. She'd make a dinner of gougères and ice cream at nine at night, if the mood struck. Or she'd play a marathon of old Joni Mitchell at top volume. Not that she'd ever give up her current life, but living alone had had its advantages.

She kicked off her shoes and settled on the chaise longue, feet pulled up, to think. Pepper jumped up next to her and rubbed his ears on her shoulder, apparently having forgiven her for the trip to the vet. Tonight, she'd have to tell Paul about her call to Crisp, but for now, she could relax. At last, her breath settled. She was reaching for a 1930s *Harper Bazaar* when Paul's truck pulled in the driveway.

"You're home already," she said with a touch of irritation.

He paused in the doorway. "That's okay with you, right?"

She sighed. "I'm happy to see you. I really am."

He shifted a bag of groceries to his other arm. Gemma wagged at his feet. "I thought I'd surprise you with dinner. One of the guys at the job site brought in salmon from a fishing trip at the coast."

"Sorry I sounded cranky. I'm just decompressing." She rose and kissed his cheek.

"What's wrong?" he asked.

She followed him to the kitchen and told him about her run-in with Stroden's sister that morning. "You should have heard her. It was awful. The first time I'd seen her, she'd been so quiet and sweet. Then this."

"You don't think she's overcompensating, do you? Faking it?"

Mary Pat's words had stung enough that Joanna hadn't thought the sister might be hiding something. She drew back. "She sounded genuine. She was nearly hysterical."

"She'd be hysterical if she'd killed her brother," he said.

A car pulled up in front of the house. Gemma ran to the window and nosed aside the lace panels but didn't bark.

"Uncle Gene," Paul said. "It's about time he showed up."

Joanna arrived at the window in time to see an older sedan pull away with what might have been a woman—or a small man—at the driver's wheel.

"This is awkward," she said.

"I suppose I'd better say something about the earrings."

"Hush. Here he comes."

Joanna and Paul were waiting for Gene when he came through the door.

"How's tricks?" Gene said. He patted each of them on his way to the kitchen, where he slid a pie pan onto the counter. "I brought us some dessert. How do you like peach-blueberry pie?"

Joanna shot Paul a glance. They had to talk to him. Gene was Paul's uncle. It would be better if he started the conversation.

Gene started humming "I Dream of Jeannie With the Light Brown Hair." "You don't have a little extra for dinner for me tonight, do you?"

Joanna glanced at Paul again and cleared her throat. "We're having salmon. There's plenty."

"I'll just go downstairs and drop off my things. I'll be up in a minute. You can assign me clean-up duty." He skipped down the steps as lightly as Fred Astaire, Gemma at his heels.

Paul squeezed Joanna's hand. "I'll talk to him."

When Gene returned to the kitchen, neither Joanna nor Paul had moved.

Gene froze, and his smile faded. "What?" The smile returned, and his shoulders relaxed. "You were wondering where I was, is that it? A gentleman never kisses and tells."

From the strain on Paul's face, Joanna knew this wasn't easy for him. Uncle Gene had been like a father to him, even if the skills he'd imparted had to do more with breaching security systems than becoming an Eagle Scout.

Paul stood straighter. "We found some emerald and diamond earrings in the basement."

Joanna appreciated the "we."

Gene's smile disappeared once again. He pulled out a dining room chair and sat. "So, that's it, huh?" His gaze fell on the earthenware vase of daisies at the center of the table. He drew himself up and turned to Joanna and Paul.

"Yes, I do know about them. And, yes, they're stolen."

Paul sat next to him. "You told us you had gone clean, that you weren't breaking into houses anymore. And then you bring stolen property into our home?"

"I told you the truth, I haven't touched anything that's not mine since I was sentenced. Honest. Well, except the Greffulhe jewels. That's what they're called." He stared toward the basement stairs. "There's a necklace and brooch, too."

"That's plenty," Paul said. "I suppose you knew where they were the whole time you were in prison, and you were waiting to get out and steal them back?"

"No. Not true."

"Stealing from another crook is still stealing, and the jewelry still belongs to someone else. If the police find out they're here, and that we've known about them, both Joanna and I stand to go to jail." His voice picked up heat.

Gene grasped his temples with his hands, mussing his carefully brilliantined hair. "Listen. Can you listen to me just a second?"

Joanna took a chair, too. This would be good.

"Honey, you might want a martini for this," Gene said.

"I'm okay, but thanks." She didn't want to move.

Gene dropped his hands to his lap. "Here's the story. Yes, the jewels are stolen. Yes, I stole them."

"You told us—" Paul began.

Gene held up a hand. "I'm not finished. It was a crime of opportunity, and I was the only one of the gang in on it. By chance, I had a solid alibi. I didn't have a buyer lined up. I figured at some point I'd break them down and sell the stones separately. Until then, it was my savings account."

A groan escaped Joanna. "Take out the gemstones? They're so gorgeous as earrings."

"It's the only way he'd be able to sell them. The collection is probably too well known," Paul said.

"That's it," Gene said.

"So you hung onto them for forty-plus years," Joanna said without thinking. Uh oh. This was not the time to casually bring up her call to Crisp.

She had Gene's full attention. "How'd you know that?"

"Just a guess," she said hurriedly. "I mean, I hadn't read in the paper about any big jewel heist, and you made it sound like it was a long time ago."

"What's your plan?" Paul asked his uncle without waiting a beat. "You must have a plan. You don't expect to carry around a fortune in jewelry the rest of your life."

"My plan is to get the jewels back to their owner."

"What?" Joanna said.

"It is?" Paul said simultaneously.

"Yes. I'm through with crime. I want the jewels returned."

Joanna was speechless. Paul, also seemingly devoid of words, laid his hands on the table. At last, Joanna found her voice. "So, you need to return the jewels without revealing that you stole them in the first place."

"Right. But I've only been out for a few months, and I'm still on papers. I've been a bit distracted. I haven't figured out the angle."

"Why not just turn them in to the police? Wouldn't that be easiest?" Joanna said.

Paul and Gene both raised their eyebrows. "Easiest one-way ticket back to prison," Paul said.

"Why is that?"

"Like I said, I'm on papers. Parole," Gene explained. "Anything that smells of crime could send me back to the joint."

Joanna could take the jewelry to the police herself, making an excuse about finding it mixed in with some vintage clothing, but it would take a smart detective half a cup of coffee and two minutes on the computer to discover that a jewel thief lived in her basement. No, they needed help who knew the law and would keep their secret. Help like Foster Crisp.

Gemma loped to the kitchen and started banging her bowl on the floor, a sign that dinner was overdue.

Gene sighed. "I'm sorry. I'm putting you kids in a spot. I didn't mean for you to find the jewels. Now that you know they're here—"

"We're at risk, too, remember," Paul finished.

This was no lie, yet Joanna felt bad for him. "You said your alibi was solid."

"Funny. I'd set up the alibi for another reason completely, but it ended up serving me better than I'd planned."

"A woman," Paul said. He turned to Joanna. "Uncle Gene was kind of a player."

"A gentleman—"

"Never kisses and tells," Joanna finished. "She doesn't happen to be an accomplished baker, does she? Your taste seems to run in that direction."

"No comment."

"I hope she knows how to bake a file into a cake, because if we don't figure out how to solve this problem, you're going back to prison," Paul said.

She had an idea. Or the spark of one, anyway. Maybe she didn't need to rush to tell Paul about her conversation with Crisp just yet.

Chapter 11

The morning dawned clear and promised another day of batting a hand fan and bemoaning Old Blue's lack of A/C. While it was still cool, Paul had left for work, and Joanna had used the morning rush as an excuse to delay telling him about Foster Crisp. She would have more to share later, anyway.

Joanna had an hour until her next appointment, so she stopped by Tallulah's Closet to check in. If things were quiet, she'd nip into the back room to talk with Auntie V. She had a lot to work out.

Apple must have brought in her own records to the store today, because Joanna arrived to French cancan music. At least half a dozen women—a crowd for Tallulah's Closet—wandered the store touching dresses and closing their eyes. It was Helen Keller at the cabaret times six.

"What's going on?"

Apple gestured for her to come closer to the tiki bar, where she sat quietly amid the rollicking music and wandering women.

"Friends. I hope you don't mind."

"Of course not. What are they doing?"

One of the women held a red and gold brocade sheath dress to her torso. Her eyes snapped open, and a smile broke over her face.

Without saying a word, Apple pointed toward the dressing room.

"They're buying dresses for a ritual. We thought wearing vintage would be a good way to get in touch with our ancestors."

Joanna accepted Apple's paganism without asking a lot of questions, but a ritual that demanded sixty-year-old cocktail dresses deserved further investigation. "I thought the ancestors you were interested in wore, oh, medieval capes or something."

"And rode brooms?" Apple's low voice could hardly be heard over the frantic music. "Ancestors can be anyone who's died." She tilted her head. "Think of your grandmother. You still hear her voice, don't you?"

Joanna did. Her grandmother's aphorisms flitted through her consciousness daily. Just this morning when trying to decide when to tell Paul about her conversation with Crisp, she'd heard, "Trouble, like fresh bread, only gets harder when you wait to cut it."

"I'm giving them the friends and family discount. I hope you don't mind," Apple said. "How are things?"

"What do you mean?"

"You've seemed distracted the past few days."

"The Stroden murder has been on my mind. I went to his house to check about the clothes again —"

"And see if anything new had turned up, I bet."

"Busted." Joanna gave a weak smile. "Stroden's sister ran me out, saying I'd killed her brother. Plus, Paul's uncle is still hanging out in our basement, raising a whole bunch of complications I'd rather not get into right now."

Joanna's reply was interrupted as Apple's friend emerged from the dressing room in the brocade sheath and bare feet. Her wavy, prematurely gray hair wafted in a halo. She looked ready for a photo shoot in an avant-garde magazine.

"Fabulous," Joanna said. "The dress fits like it was made for her, too."

Another of Apple's friends went into a dressing room with a 1940s rayon day dress in a back-to-school print of books and apples.

"I sense it's more than that," Apple said. Sometimes when Apple looked at her, Joanna felt like her skull had grown a television screen with one channel: her feelings. Apple was looking at her this way now. "Are things okay with Paul?"

"Of course," Joanna replied before Apple had finished speaking.

"I know marriage can be tough. Paul seems easygoing, but, if you don't mind my saying so, you can be tightly wound. I wonder if you've had trouble talking with him?"

"About what?" Joanna asked. About calling out his uncle's grand larceny to an ex-cop, for instance?

"I don't know. You used to be super-focused on the shop. These days, you're more interested in running down murder suspects. Just yesterday I showed you a Josef of Hollywood bib necklace a customer dropped off, and you barely registered it."

Apple was right. It was a glorious necklace and deserved a closer look. "Where is it, anyway?"

"Never mind." Apple rested her fists on her hips. "You're not going to tell me, are you?"

"I will. Just not this second." She watched one of Apple's friends smile and clip on an earring, then yank it off with a grimace.

Casting around for something to change the subject, Joanna asked, "What's this music about? I'd have thought you'd be listening to some kind of witchy New Age thing." She picked up the album cover with Zsa Zsa Gabor cavorting in a gay nineties dress. "It's the soundtrack to *Moulin Rouge*."

"Colette writes spells with *Moulin Rouge*—the new version—playing on the TV in the background. I couldn't find that one on vinyl.

You're avoiding my question, by the way. Don't think I didn't notice."

Joanna set the album cover back on top of the stereo. "You're right. I don't know what's going on with me. I still love the shop, I do. But the Stroden murder won't leave me alone. And Gene. Like I said, I can't talk about it right now."

"Can't talk about it with me, maybe, but don't forget Paul."

"Oh, we've discussed Gene. Just this morning, in fact."

"What about the murder? Have you talked about that with Paul? I don't mean just about the facts, but about your fascination with it. In a marriage, that's part of your job—and a big part of the benefits."

"Kind of. A bit." *Trouble, like fresh bread...*

Apple stared at her, then apparently deciding she wouldn't get more of a response, picked up the bag from Stamp Gurlz. "What's with all the rubber stamps? They're great. We should stamp the price tags with them."

An older woman wearing a Princess Diana style fascinator—Joanna had hesitated when she picked it up at an estate sale, but seeing it on she was glad she'd made the purchase—seemed to materialize at the tiki bar.

"You're Joanna, yes?" Her voice was delicate but somehow cut cleanly through the music. "Apple talks about you."

"That's me. I hope you're enjoying the shop. Anything I can help you with?"

"You're at a crossroads. Aren't you?"

The woman's gaze seemed both faraway, yet focused on Joanna. The white feather on her fascinator bobbed as she spoke.

"I'm not sure what you mean."

She squinted, as if looking beyond her. "You'd better watch out, honey." Her eyes narrowed further, and she pulled back her head.

"The garden."

"Garden? You mean, flowers and grass?"

The woman shrugged. "That's it. That's all I've got. Feet and a garden."

The record came to an abrupt ending, the turntable's needle making a rhythmic rasp. Joanna went to lift the arm, and when she turned again, the woman was on the other side of the boutique, examining a pair of pink patent leather slides.

"That was Marta," Apple said. "She's an herbalist, and she doesn't get many intuitive flashes. But when she does, you'd better listen."

Chapter 12

Joanna shifted Old Blue out of park and thought about the scene she'd just left at Tallulah's Closet. What had the witch meant by "crossroads"? Sure, she was asking a few questions about Bradley Stroden's death. She wasn't anywhere near action that could lead to trouble. Then there was Gene's situation. There, she was definitely taking action that might lead to trouble. She was about to make it worse.

Foster Crisp lived in Portland's Sellwood neighborhood, not far from Joanna. Somehow that surprised her, although there was no reason she should know anything about his personal life—despite what he knew about hers, having seen her through a number of harrowing situations over the past few years. He'd told her he'd been raised on a ranch in Eastern Oregon, and he dressed the part in cowboy boots and bolo ties. He'd mentioned his wife. He'd been well respected in the police force up through his retirement the spring before. That was really all she knew.

She parked in front of a modest bungalow fringed with azaleas and rhododendrons that must have fired up a postcard-worthy display in spring. The porch was freshly swept. She rang the doorbell.

A woman in stretchy pants and a Portland Camellia Association T-shirt answered the door. "You must be Joanna. Foster's expecting you." She turned toward the rear of the house. "Honey? She's here."

His and hers tan recliners with afghans over their backs faced a television set. Family photos rested on side tables. The only note of color was a vase of garden roses on the coffee table.

"Good to see you." Crisp had emerged from the hall and offered his hand. No cowboy boots or western shirt today. Just stockinged feet and a red Pendleton Rodeo T-shirt. "Come on back."

Crisp had taken over one of the rear bedrooms as his office. Here, too, decor was spare, but the window let out to a view of a soft lawn and flower beds in orange and pink. A scrub jay splashed in the birdbath.

Joanna sat in what she suspected was a chair left over from a dinette set donated to Goodwill long ago. "Thanks for meeting with me."

"My pleasure." He sat at the office chair at his desk and waited for her to continue.

"It's about Paul's Uncle Gene."

No raised eyebrow, no dropped jaw. "You want to turn him in?"

"No." The word came out more loudly than she'd expected. "No, that's not it. I want to help him. You're a private investigator now. I want to hire you."

He leaned back in his chair. "This is an interesting turn of events. You know I helped put him away the first time he went to prison, right?"

"I know. But you're also fair."

Crisp clasped hands over his belt buckle. "Tell me more."

She wasn't that stupid. "I won't tell you anything until you've agreed to work for me. Once I'm your client, you're bound by confidentiality, right?"

"Does this have to do with the Greffulhe jewels?"

Joanna pressed her lips together and stared at him.

He let out his breath. "Okay. Give me a dollar."

"What?"

"If you want to be my client, you have to pay me."

Joanna fumbled through her purse—this one a red leather bag tooled with an Aztec motif—for her wallet. "I have a five."

Crisp snatched the bill and tucked it under his keyboard. "There. You're my client. It doesn't mean I can actually do anything for you until I hear what's going on. What's the story?"

"If I tell you something that might implicate someone else, too, is that person protected?"

"Like, for instance, Gene?"

"Answer me, please." Outside, the scrub jay squawked at a sparrow, then fluttered out of the birdbath to a tree studded with plums.

"If it has to do with a crime you might be accused of, then yes."

Her shoulders relaxed. "Then, sure, it's about the jewels. And, yes, Gene hid them in our basement."

"I knew it. I knew he heisted those jewels." Crisp shook his head, then laughed and slapped his knee. "That S.O.B. I wonder how he finagled his alibi?" He shook his head again. "Why do you need my help? I assume he's planning to fence the jewels now, or do it when his parole is over and take off for Mexico. I'm not sure how a private investigator figures in."

"According to him, he wants to return the jewels. Says this is the last thing he has to do before his old life is completely behind him. I believe him. He can't figure out how to do it without getting into trouble. That's why I need your help." Not only would Gene then have moved on from crime, maybe he'd even get his own apartment—or move in with the baker.

"Well, we could package them up and give them to the police. Let them take care of it." Joanna was about to speak, but he cut in. "I know what you're going to say, and you're right. They might reopen the investigation, and it wouldn't be too hard to draw a line from me to you to Gene."

"Could we return them anonymously to the woman they were stolen from?"

"That has risks, too. Besides, I don't even know if she's alive. It's a possibility, though." He drummed his fingers on the chair's arm. "Let me think about it and get back to you. I'll do some poking around."

"There's one more thing."

"About Gene?"

"No. This actually has to do with your old career in homicide. It's about Bradley Stroden." Joanna clasped her purse, then released it. "I was wondering if you could give me an idea of how the investigation would go. You know, in general."

For the first time today, a hint of Crisp's old presence as a detective came back. His body seemed to come to full attention. "Why do you want to know?"

"I was there when he died. Naturally, I'm curious."

"Naturally. Naturally, you're more curious than most. But there's something more, isn't there?"

She didn't know herself why it was so important to her to figure out who murdered Stroden. Sure, part of it was because she was there when he died. Part of it was the possibility of getting her hands on an Edith Head-designed movie wardrobe. And some of it was to refute his sister's accusation that she was the killer. Joanna had learned she had a knack for pulling out the emotional threads of a murder case. The police and their labs and databases could uncover a lot, but she had a nose for figuring out the "why." And she'd discovered she liked it.

"Like you said, I'm curious," she said.

Sounds of cupboard doors opening came from the kitchen. It would be time for dinner soon.

"The Stroden case. Well, the results of the autopsy should be in by now."

"Poisoning. I'm sure. He'd just eaten a violet candy from a tin that had come in the mail."

"They will have tested that, then, and traced the package."

"That's the thing. The package disappeared. If the pastille Stroden had just given me hadn't fallen on the floor, they wouldn't have had anything to test." She tapped a finger on her purse. "But what about the thought process? How would they decide what leads to follow?"

"If it were my case, and I was sure the crime was premeditated, I'd want to know why he was killed. I'd look for a motive."

"That was my thought, too," Joanna said. "The detective on the case, Roscoe, pooh-poohed that approach. He says he looks at means and opportunity."

"Roscoe's new in homicide. He has his own methods. You've been thinking about motive, though. What have you come up with?"

"Stroden was writing his memoir." Joanna had already been through this. "Maybe someone thought he was planning to reveal something in particular. Something incriminating."

"Then, if it were my case, I'd want to see the memoir, and I'd want to know who knew he was writing it."

"That makes sense. Connected to that, I wonder…could he have been blackmailing someone?"

"You mean, threatening he'd tell a story unless he was paid off? That would answer the other question I'd ask, which would be 'why now'?"

"So, for motive we have"—Joanna raised her index finger—"one, Stroden was planning to reveal a story; and, two"—her middle finger joined the first—"he threatened to reveal a story unless the subject of the story paid him."

"Blackmail is always a strong motive, but I'd look first at who inherits," Crisp said.

"His sister, Mary Pat. Stroden's secretary says they're broke."

"This dovetails with the question I always ask, which is, why now? Why kill Stroden now, instead of next year or ten years ago?"

Joanna nodded. "The memoir. What else could it be?"

"Then I'd ask, what's in the memoir that is so juicy that someone would kill if it were released?"

"I talked with him about the memoir for only a few minutes. He mentioned a movie he'd worked on—*Starlit Wonder*—and how he was going to shake up Hollywood with the story."

Crisp tapped his desk with a pencil. "If Stroden was blackmailing someone, he was making money. Did he have any outstanding bills? You say he'd borrowed against his house. Had he made any large purchases?"

"Unless he'd made the blackmail request but hadn't been paid off yet," she pointed out. "As a P.I., can you investigate his finances?"

"I thought you were hiring me to return the Greffulhe jewels."

Joanna pressed her lips together a moment. "Just asking. Like I said, Luke, Stroden's secretary, said he was broke. A peek at his bank balance would clear it up."

"There's your motivation." Through the window beyond Crisp, a second bird splashed in the birdbath. "To answer your question, no. I don't have that kind of access. But, this secretary. Just how much does he know about this memoir?"

She shrugged. "Presumably, everything. He took dictation and typed it up."

Crisp leaned back and folded his arms. "Then he has plenty of information to send letters of his own. You might have your blackmailer right there."

Chapter 13

"Say Bradley Stroden wasn't murdered because of blackmail or the inheritance," Joanna said. "What other reasons might there be?"

"Honey, dinner's about ready." Crisp's wife appeared at the door, her face flushed from heat. "Would you like to stay? It's not fancy, but there's enough chicken Caesar salad for all of us."

"Thank you, but I should be getting home. Paul's expecting me."

"I'll be out in a minute, June." Then, to Joanna, "I wouldn't discount the secretary. Who else had access to his memoir?"

"His sister could have read it." Joanna was already plotting a return to the Stroden mansion. This time she'd come prepared to meet up with his grief-stricken sister.

Crisp rose. The sun slanted low over the back lawn now, streaking it with long shadows. "Don't worry about it. I guarantee you this is a line the police are following up on. They have more tools than I do. Access to bank accounts, for one. If there's blackmailing involved, they'll get to the bottom of it."

⁑

Watching Paul and his uncle cooking dinner side by side, each wearing one of her vintage aprons, was a pleasure. She might as well savor it a moment before she dropped her bomb.

"The thing with goulash," Gene said, "is that you've got to be choosy about your paprika. Not too sweet, not too spicy. And fresh. It pays to get the real stuff from Hungary." He wiped his hands on his turquoise apron with its pattern of tiny hearts.

"I'd ask you where you learned that, but I have a feeling I'd get that line about kissing and telling." Paul was dicing a pile of carrots and onions. His apron was mustard colored with pink rickrack trim and a pattern of brown clovers.

"A gentleman never does," Gene replied.

"So I've heard," Paul said.

Their banter was easy, comfortable. She could imagine when Paul was in high school and Gene taught him to use the tools he was expert with now. More sawdust, less old calico.

"I have an announcement," she said.

"Pink is the navy blue of India," Gene said.

A Diana Vreeland quote. "Where did you hear that?"

"A gentleman never kisses and tells," said Paul and Gene at the same time.

Gene tossed cubes of pork into the iron skillet. They hissed as they hit the hot fat.

Joanna laughed. "No, as serious as that is, this is even more important." Despite herself, her heart beat a bit faster and she felt her face pinkening. "I hired a private investigator this afternoon."

Gene turned off the heat and pulled the skillet off the burner. "What?"

Paul set down his knife and turned, too.

She swallowed. "To help us figure out how to get the Greffuhle jewels back to their owner. I told you I'd help solve this."

The silence that greeted her reply had more force than shouting would have. Standing next to each other, Paul and Gene's family resemblance was plain. So was their apparent feeling that no one but family should be involved in family trouble.

"Oh, no," Paul said.

"What?" Joanna said. "We need help. We need to know our options and the least risky legal path."

Gene shook his head. "This is my problem to solve. Bringing an outsider into it opens the door to more trouble. No. No good can come of this."

Joanna stood. "That's the thing. It isn't just your problem anymore. You brought stolen property into my house—"

"Our house," Paul said.

"Yes." A second passed, then two. Her voice faltered. "Our house. Now we're all at risk." Pepper rubbed against her legs. Joanna picked him up. "It's my problem, too. So I hired help to solve it."

Paul shot a glance at his uncle. "I wish you would have talked to me about it first."

Joanna forged ahead. "The P.I. I hired—it's Foster Crisp."

"Oh, no," Gene said, and Paul groaned.

"No, listen. It's good. If I'm his client, he can't divulge anything I tell him that might incriminate me."

"I was the thief, not you," Gene said.

"I know, but you're protected by association, since Paul's and my crime is knowing about—and harboring—stolen property without reporting it."

"She has a point," Paul said. Slowly, he returned to chopping vegetables.

"Crisp was all right with this?" Gene asked.

"He wanted to know how you pulled off the original heist with such a solid alibi, but, yes, he took the case."

Paul reached past his uncle and put the skillet back on the burner. Sensible man. Whatever else happened, they had to eat.

"What's next, then?"

"He's looking into who would have inherited the jewels and thinking things through. He said he'd get back to us." She raised her gaze to Paul's. He looked away. Pepper wriggled to be let down.

"I guess Crisp is an okay guy," Gene said. "He's a man of his word, anyway. If he says he won't turn me in, he won't."

"He promised," Joanna said and sincerely hoped he'd meant it.

Chapter 14

Joanna dawdled at her bath, but she couldn't stay in the tub forever. By unspoken agreement, she, Paul, and Gene hadn't talked about Crisp or the jewels at dinner, but Joanna had the feeling it was never far from any of their minds. Gene had made an excuse and left the house not long after dishes were cleared, and Paul had escaped to the garage to finish a piece of molding. He'd gone to bed early. Finally, fingers like bleached prunes, she toweled herself off, donned a kimono, and padded through the quiet house to the bedroom.

Paul was sitting up in bed, blankets puddled over his lap. He patted the sheets next to him, the silver scar on his hand catching the light.

She slid under the covers, and he turned off the bedside light. She was glad. It was easier to talk in the dark.

He waited for her to speak first.

"I saw Foster Crisp without talking to you about it," she said.

"I heard." In the dark, his voice wasn't angry or accusatory. Simply matter of fact.

Why had she visited Crisp without mentioning it to Paul? Whatever came of it would affect not just her, but Paul and Gene. Yet, without a second thought, she'd picked up the phone and dialed Crisp's number. She could tell Paul it had been habit. She'd lived alone so long that she'd forgotten that her decisions could affect others. Only a few seconds of reflection unveiled this as a lie. Who was she kidding? She remembered Paul all day, every day.

No, she'd wanted to talk to Crisp not just about Gene's problem, but about Bradley Stroden, and she'd been afraid Paul didn't want her to deepen her involvement in the murder. The fact was, she couldn't help but speculate about Stroden's death. But neither could she bear the possibility that Paul would try to stop her, and she didn't know what she'd do if he tried.

"I'm sorry," she said.

He reached over, his hand warm on her hip. "Thank you. That means a lot." He cleared his throat. "I don't pretend to be an expert, but married people should confide in each other. One person's problem is the other person's, too. I want you to know that whatever happens, we can handle it together."

She let this sink in. Marriage was new to her, and she wasn't very good at it. Not yet, anyway. She steeled herself. This must be how Olympic divers felt before the plunge. "There's something else you should know. When I went to see Crisp, it was about more than Gene's situation. I wanted to talk to him about the Stroden murder."

His hand stiffened, but his breath remained even. "Yes?"

"I love running Tallulah's Closet, but I've come to understand something about myself. It's not just the beautiful old dresses that draw me, it's their stories. I like imagining each dress's life. The best part of having a vintage clothing shop is going to estate sales and wondering about the people who lived in each house. I love seeing the tea cups they chose for everyday, the half-used bottles of perfume, the souvenirs from trips—everything." She smoothed the quilt. "I guess what I'm trying to say is that I like the puzzle. I like figuring out how lives go together and what motivates them." She lifted her gaze to his, but night shadowed his expression.

"And Bradley Stroden's murder is part of that."

"I can't help but wonder. In a way, it fuels me, and I'm good at it. But don't worry. The police have this one. I'm just a curious bystander."

From Gemma's dog bed came the quiet whimpers of her dreaming.

"Sometimes I wonder if you like being married, Jo. You still keep so much to yourself. We're a team now. You and me."

She sank lower in the bed. "I know. Maybe I haven't gotten used to having someone else on my team." She turned and clasped his arm. "Are you really on board? Even with my nosing around about Bradley Stroden?"

"You know I am," he said softly. "Just don't do anything stupid."

"I won't."

What if she relied on him and he let her down? A familiar ache sparked in her chest, but it was faint. Just a hum. Maybe soon it would go away altogether.

"You can count on me," he said. "Especially when the decision involves both of us."

The words stung. He was right. "Then I will."

He bent and kissed her. "Partner."

The next day at Tallulah's Closet, Joanna dumped out a bag of hundred-year-old French nightgowns fresh from the laundry and turned on the steamer. She plotted how she was going to talk to Luke, Stroden's secretary. The last time she'd gone to Stroden's house had turned out a disaster, with Mary Pat wailing and accusing her of murder. Remembering, she clenched her jaw.

Yes, she'd told Paul she was merely a bystander to the murder case. But Crisp had pointed out that someone else with access to Stroden's memoir could have been a blackmailer, and Luke was at the top of the list. Pretending he was Stroden, Luke might have sent out a threatening letter or two and demanded payment. One of the recipients might have preferred to kill rather than risk having his secret revealed.

It would be worth a few questions with Luke to see exactly what he knew. She could call him again and suggest he try once more to sell Stroden's clothing to her, only offsite. At the shop, for instance. That surely wouldn't qualify as doing something "stupid."

But why would Luke agree? What would he get out of it? She might hint at a cut for him if he could arrange the sale. The dresses Stroden had set aside to sell were okay and in good shape, but normally she wouldn't go to so much trouble for them. The Edith Head costumes, on the other hand…well, they were something special. Joanna would love to examine even one dress and see what tricks Head had used to make the most of the actress's figure. She still dreamed of the gold lamé gown that flowed like gilded water over Dorothy Lamour's curves in *My Favorite Brunette*.

The French nightgowns steamed out beautifully. A friend of a friend in Burgundy was a die-hard thrifter who visited the local *vide grenier* sales for relaxation. She'd amassed a huge collection of old cotton and linen nightgowns, many with their original mother-of-pearl buttons and hand embroidery, and Joanna had jumped at the chance to buy them. So many vintage dresses had tiny waists. These nightgowns were comfortably ample and would make chic chemises paired with leggings and a cardigan.

As she slipped the next nightgown on a hanger, she considered how she'd approach Luke. Could she call the house and hope Mary Pat didn't answer?

The phone rang. "Tallulah's Closet," Joanna answered, one hand still holding the steamer's wand.

"Joanna? This is Luke, Bradley Stroden's secretary. I'd hoped you'd be there."

She clicked off the steamer with a toe and spun to the phone to give it her full attention. "Yes, I'm here. I'm glad you called." Talk about kismet. No *Moulin Rouge* soundtrack necessary, either.

"Yeah, well, I wondered if you still wanted those clothes?"

"I do, but—"

"Don't worry about Mary Pat. She's out all afternoon. Could you come now?"

Business at the shop was slow. All she'd sold that morning was a striped Jantzen one-piece swimsuit to a collector from Japan. And that had been over the phone.

"I'll be right over," she said.

In the car, she realized that she should have left Paul a message telling him where she was—for both her safety and his peace of mind. Oh, well. She'd tell him all about it when she got home. That's what married people did.

Chapter 15

She couldn't help breathing more quickly as she approached the stairs to the Stroden mansion. It wasn't the climb stealing her breath, but the fact that she might be calling on a blackmailer. A blackmailer indirectly responsible for murder. She lifted her finger to the doorbell. Luke pulled open the door before she'd pushed the bell, and she stepped back.

"Sorry," she said. "I didn't expect you to answer so fast."

"Come in. I was just bringing down a suitcase." Two pieces of luggage sat to the door's right.

Luke was soberly dressed today. It crossed Joanna's mind that he might be wearing one of Stroden's old suits. The lapel was topstitched by hand, and the fact that Luke hadn't buttoned the vest suggested it had been tailored for someone with a tighter waist—or a corset.

She followed him in. The scent of violets was nearly gone, but Stroden's personality still infused every corner. She wondered what Mary Pat planned to do with the house, if she'd even be able to keep up with the property taxes.

Luke led her through the dining area to the morning room. The clothing she'd chosen on her last visit was packed into five grocery bags stacked against the wall. She recognized the lavender ruffle of one dress and the mint green sleeve of another.

"Since you've already seen the clothes, I put them in bags. Why don't we say five hundred for the lot?" Luke said.

She could probably sell them for a thousand dollars, over six months or so. With rent, paying Apple, and other operating expenses, she needed a larger margin. "How about three-fifty?" Even that was a push. These styles were off-market.

"All right. Three-fifty, then." He was quick to respond. Too quick.

"Obviously, I can't write the check to Mr. Stroden."

"You couldn't do cash?"

"I'd need to go to the bank." She hesitated. "How about if I write the check to you? Or Mary Pat?"

"Why don't you leave that line blank? I'll fill it in later."

Her hand paused mid-reach for her checkbook. He planned to make off with this money, she was sure. "Maybe I'd better write it to you. For my records." She wasn't going to get involved in stealing a dead man's clothes. "You can always sign it over to Mary Pat later. What's your last name?"

"Brock. Luke Brock." He was already moving the bags of clothing to the entry hall.

She ripped the check from the book and set it on the table next to a pile of the day's mail. "Speaking of Mary Pat, I brought her this." She pulled a small padded-velvet Victorian scrapbook from her bag. "It was probably meant for autographs, but I thought it would make a nice memory book. There's a card inside. I feel awful about my last visit."

"Thanks. I'll give it to her." He set the book on the side table. "Don't worry about Mary Pat. She hasn't said a word about it since. She was kind of emotional, that's all."

"She seemed worse than that."

"Like I said, don't sweat it. She's fine."

He was already hustling her out the door, and she hadn't even been in the house ten minutes.

"One more thing. Do you think I could take a peek at the Edith Head costumes? You were going to show them to me last time when we were interrupted." As he showed her the costumes, she'd try again to quiz him on the memoir. It would buy her time and give her a look at the wardrobe.

He lifted another two bags and shook his head. "I don't know."

She followed him to the entry hall. "I came so close to seeing them last time. I admit, I've been dreaming about those costumes ever since."

He set down the bags. "I'm afraid I can't. I have somewhere I have to be. These are the last two bags of clothes. You can take them to your car while I finish up a few things here."

She looked at him blankly. He wasn't even going to help? "It will take a couple of trips."

"I'll leave the front door open."

"Luke," she said firmly.

He turned to face her. "What?"

"Why are you in such a hurry to leave? You knew I was coming. You called to set it up."

"Why are you so eager to stick around?" he countered.

"You have on Mr. Stroden's suit, don't you?"

He looked down at his torso, as if he didn't know what he was wearing.

When he didn't respond, she nodded. "And you can't get rid of me—or collect my money—fast enough. What's going on?"

"I hope you aren't insinuating anything." He stepped closer. His breath wafted the sour tang of sugared coffee. "If you're smart, you'll take your clothes and leave." He leaned back and folded his arms across his chest. "You were the last person to see Bradley alive, you know."

Oh, she knew that. "Yes—"

"I might have heard you yelling at him. In fact, I think I did. Mary Pat couldn't have. She was in the kitchen. But I might have been in the hall when you threatened Bradley. Then, poisoned him."

"That's insane. I—"

"It's your word against mine, isn't it?"

Anger burned through her arteries. She didn't dare look at him, that blackmailer. Yes, blackmailer. Now she was sure.

"Remember what Mary Pat said. You killed her brother. She'd back me up."

Joanna stepped back and fought to steady her breath. Five bags sat side by side on the entry hall's polished parquet floor. So, that was it. No further info about the memoir. Not even a peek at the Edith Head costumes. No, all she'd come out of this with were a threat and five bags of clothing that would take ages to sell.

"Fine," she said through gritted teeth.

"Not even a thank you?" he practically sneered. "We probably won't meet again. I'm off to New York for a few months. I can't take another rainy winter, anyway."

"I'll be out of here in a few minutes, and you can catch your flight."

Luke saluted her from the doorway and headed toward the morning room, probably to stash the check she'd written him in his wallet ASAP.

She loaded a bag in each arm, took the stairs down to Old Blue, and stuffed them in. She looked up to the house, two flights of concrete steps from the street, and started the climb again. No wonder Stroden had been so thin.

As she took the steps, she pondered their hasty meeting. Luke sure was eager to get out of town. And so suddenly. Why? She picked up the next two bags of clothes. The police must have ruled him out as a suspect—or witness—to let him move out of state so soon. That is, if they knew about his plans.

She heaved the bags into the Corolla's hatchback and returned to the stairs, with a quick glance to see if the neighbor was watching again. The curtains remained still.

Luke had wanted cash, but had happily snatched the check as long as she'd written it out to him. Mary Pat wouldn't take it well if she discovered Joanna had been buying her brother's things and paying Luke. Maybe Joanna should send a note thanking her and letting her know that Luke had the check.

Then there was Luke's threat of fingering her as the murderer. He could flourish her check to the police and say it was a bribe to keep him quiet.

She wanted a receipt, and she wanted out of there. She had to think.

"Luke?" she called out in the entry hall, a sack of shoes and hats in her hand.

He didn't answer. The grandfather clock in the hall chimed the quarter hour, nearly causing her to drop the bag. She glanced toward the street. No sign of Mary Pat returning. No anybody. Relax, she told herself.

She raised her voice. "Luke?" Maybe he went through to the kitchen. Probably a servant's staircase led upstairs where his bedroom was. She'd try calling out just one more time, then she was going home, never to see his nasty face again.

She set down the clothing and passed through the dining room. Her steps made no noise on the rose-patterned rug.

She turned to the morning room. "Luke? Would it be too much trouble to get a receipt? I know you—"

She froze at the doorway. Luke was there, all right. At the table, face down, an opened letter in his hand and a cup of coffee next to him. She touched Luke's shoulder, jiggled it, and drew back her arm. Words froze in her mouth.

It was a week to the day that Stroden had died. Two dead bodies in seven days.

Chapter 16

Joanna's breath caught in her chest. She pressed two fingers on the warm skin of Luke's neck. Nothing. She'd never been very good at reading a pulse. She reached for his hand, then pulled back. Bradley Stroden had been poisoned. Luke appeared to have been reading a letter when he died, a letter that might also have been poisoned. A half-drunk cup of coffee sat at his elbow, too.

Calm dropped over her like a chiffon veil. She wasn't sure if the house had a landline, but Luke's phone was facedown on the table. She picked it up and was confronted with a prompt for a passcode. She set the phone aside and hurried in search of a house phone.

A central area, like the hall, was her first choice, but there was no phone there. She'd have seen it. She passed through the hall and parlor to the library. Her breath was measured, her thinking even, but her fingers felt cold. On the desk sat a classic Bakelite phone with a dial. She silently thanked Stroden for his old school sense of style. She lifted the heavy receiver and dialed 9-1-1.

As the dispatcher answered, her gaze fell on a drawer that was ajar. "Yes," she told the dispatcher, "there's been an emergency. We need an ambulance right away. And the police."

She gave the address and hung up the phone. Should she sit near Luke? It didn't matter now. The house was dead silent. Her eyes returned to the desk drawer. Using her skirt to mask her fingers, she nudged the drawer open further. There it was, a fat bundle of double-spaced pages. "Scandals Between the Scenes," the title page read.

This was it. The memoir. She glanced through the arch to the parlor. She was alone. In a minute, the police would be here. Again using her skirt, she lifted the manuscript and opened it to the middle. Marks in blue pen crossed off one whole paragraph with Joan Crawford's name in it. The next page was paper-clipped and Callie Rampton's name was circled along with David Sipriano's—the Big Sip. Interesting. Joanna opened the manuscript deeper in, looking for a mention of *Starlit Wonder*. There were no marks here—perhaps Stroden hadn't edited this far before he died. She flipped to the last page. It ended mid-story. He hadn't yet finished.

A grating sound caught her ear, and she dropped the manuscript to the drawer and pushed it shut with her knee. Except for the sound of her pulse pounding in her ears, she heard nothing. Must have been a branch rubbing against the window, or the creaks of an old house settling.

A siren in the distance grew closer. She rubbed her palms against her cheeks and took a deep breath, then crossed to the entry hall to wait. Within seconds, an ambulance pulled up on the street below with a fire engine close behind.

"Up here," she shouted. Two firemen ran up the stairs. "The last room on the right."

Through the arched doorways she saw the taller man push Luke's head back while the other man knelt at his side. She fell onto a stiff chair in the entry hall. Curiously, the smell of violets seemed to intensify. She closed her eyes and opened them a moment later to more uniformed people lugging a portable gurney. Right behind them was Detective Roscoe, his gray curly hair more frantic than ever.

"Well, well. If it isn't the vintage clothing lady. Two visits, two bodies. That's quite a record."

"I was meeting Mr. Stroden's secretary when—"

Behind the detective, Stroden's sister elbowed the detective aside, her face white with emotion. Joanna tensed. Here it would come, another barrage of yelling.

Instead, Mary Pat collapsed on the floor in tears.

"I had an appointment," Joanna said. She and Detective Roscoe stood in a puddle of sunlight cast through the library windows.

"As you did last time, if I remember right," the detective replied in a tone of voice that indicated that he did, in fact, remember right.

"No, really—"

The detective took her elbow and steered her to a chair. "Start at the beginning."

She told him about her call from Luke—"If you don't believe me, you can trace it," she said, not knowing if this was something done only on TV—and meeting him to buy Stroden's clothes.

"Were they his to sell? Probate should just be getting started."

"He said Stroden's sister said it was all right."

"Is that so?" He'd be checking on that, she was sure.

"I loaded the car and came back to get a receipt. I found him just like that."

"That's all?" Roscoe said. "You didn't touch anything else?"

She fastened her lips and shook her head.

He stared at her a moment. "Is that all?"

"Did you know Stroden was writing his memoir when he died?"

"You've only brought it up, oh, half a dozen times."

Joanna ignored his tone. "Well, it crossed my mind that he may have been blackmailing someone. He or Luke. Stroden dictated his memoir to Luke, and he was privy to Stroden's secrets. I bet Luke blackmailed someone and pretended to be Stroden."

"You sound pretty sure."

"I asked a few questions while I was looking at the clothes, and Luke threatened me. He said that unless I backed off, he'd tell you I killed Stroden."

Roscoe nodded slowly. "So, you were asking questions, were you?"

She hesitated. "I saw a copy of the memoir. Maybe you'd like to take a look at it."

Roscoe pulled at a corkscrew curl that had lodged in his glasses. "I have a copy of the memoir on a flash drive but haven't gotten to it yet. The digital copy will tell us when sections were added to the manuscript."

"Lou?" One of the uniformed policemen yelled over the banister from upstairs. "The sister is calling for Joanna Hayworth. That's her?"

Anticipating a tongue lashing, Joanna shrank.

"Why would Stroden's sister want to talk to you?" Roscoe asked.

"I don't know. Maybe because of the dresses?" The shock of finding Luke dead that had kept her so calm was beginning to wane. Her hand trembled, and she sat on it. She wished she were anywhere but at the Stroden mansion. At the same time, she didn't want to be anywhere else.

"Really? She wants to talk to you about old dresses?"

"I don't need to go up there," Joanna said. "You probably want to talk with her first."

"You mean you don't want to go upstairs."

"She's grieving. This, after her brother? She needs professional help, not me."

Roscoe watched her without reply. A long moment passed.

"All right," Joanna said finally. "The last time I was here, Mary Pat freaked out and accused me of killing her brother. I'm not sure I'm up for more of that."

"Roscoe?" the cop upstairs yelled again. "She coming?"

"You'd better go," the detective said. "See Ms. Stroden. If it gets rough, remember there's a uniform in the hall. I'll be in touch." He turned for the morning room.

Her legs were shaky as she rose from the chair. There was no question of sneaking upstairs and tucking the manuscript under her arm now. Her bag was too small to hide it — vintage purses were marvels of craft, but generally tiny — and a fresh load of police was coming through the front door.

"Joanna, right? She keeps asking for you," a uniformed cop said from the upstairs landing.

She took a deep breath and stood straighter. "I'll be right there."

Chapter 17

"Through here," the cop said. "I'll leave you two alone. If you need me — or a doctor — just shout."

Mary Pat's room was at the far end of the house, just above the kitchen. Joanna had expected a profusion of chintz and ruffles, but Mary Pat's bedroom was plain. A practical Berber carpet covered the oak floors. The only ornate touch was the portrait of an elaborately mustachioed Victorian man hanging over the marble fireplace.

Mary Pat lay propped up by pillows on a mid-century maple bed with a matching nightstand on one side and desk on the other. A bay window let in eastern light bright with the August morning.

"You wanted to see me?"

"Joanna?" Mary Pat said. "Sit here." She pointed to the end of her bed. Pink rimmed her eyes, and the creases on her cheeks had deepened.

Warily, Joanna sat, purse in lap.

"I'm sorry for exploding at you like I did the other day. My brother — my last family member — had died, and I guess I just couldn't keep it together. I blamed you. That wasn't right."

"I understand. You'd had a gigantic shock."

"I owe you an explanation."

"Oh, no. Anyone would have —"

"Listen." Her feather pillow sighed as Mary Pat leaned back. "Not a lot of people know this, but I'm actually Bradley's older sister. My mother"— Mary Pat raised an eyebrow —"you've seen her portrait downstairs?"

Joanna nodded. "The woman in the cloche hat?" With the sour expression and wire-thin lips? she wanted to add.

"Mother was disappointed in me. She'd wanted a boy, someone to replace her own father."

Joanna followed her gaze to the painting next to the window. Mary Pat's grandfather. "That's him."

"Yes. Grandpa Edwin. He died before I was born, but I feel a kinship with him. We both lived to serve my mother, although in different ways." Mary Pat was somewhere else now. She absently reached for the water glass. "Bradley and my mother were inseparable. Even when he was a boy, he helped choose her wardrobe and went with her to bridge parties. Meanwhile, I stayed home and, when they were home, too, found refuge in the garden." Her hand replaced the glass and touched a clutch of asters next to the decanter.

Mary Pat must have followed Joanna's turn toward the narrow garden, because she said, "It wasn't always like that."

"The garden, you mean?"

She nodded. "Bradley was—I hate to speak ill of him, he was my brother—but, well, he was extravagant. And not always a consistent worker. We had to sell off the back part of the garden."

"That must have been hard on you."

"Bradley said it had to be done, so it had to be done. Mother's bones would have combusted in her grave had she known we'd sold the house. So we sold off most of the land."

"So, you and Bradley weren't very close," Joanna said.

"What makes you think that?" Her eyes widened in surprise. "No, we were very close. We needed each other more than ever. Bradley loved Mother, but he wanted to get away. She was pressing him to get married, and, well." She extended a hand, palm up, as if serving an unspoken explanation. "Anyway, we went to Hollywood. At least, Bradley went to Hollywood, and Mother insisted I go along. Someone had to take care of him, she said."

"So you went."

"I went," she repeated. "At first, I was bored. Bradley was out at all hours, and I sat alone in our apartment—it was so blazing hot that first summer—and played solitaire and listened to Rosemary Clooney records. I did Bradley's laundry and made dinner for him. I resented Mother for making me go, but not enough that I didn't long to return home." She let a hand drop to the coverlet. "That all changed soon enough."

"How?"

"I was at the laundromat, when a gentleman approached me, said I ought to give a screen test. He said I had a Mary Pickford look."

Come to think of it, Joanna thought, she did. Mary Pat's color was returning. She even showed a bare smile.

"Pickford was decades out of style then," Mary Pat said. "He told me it was time for a resurgence, that the bombshell was overplayed. So, without telling Bradley, I did the test. The studio signed me."

"What did your brother say?"

She laughed, the morning's shock momentarily forgotten. "I was afraid he'd be livid. He was supposed to be the important one, not me. But he loved it. He even gave me my stage name, Margay." She pronounced the name as if offering a spray of lilies of the valley. "Margay."

"Did you have a lot of roles?"

She shrugged. "A few. It didn't last long, though." She raised her gaze to Joanna's, then looked quickly away. "I fell in love, but that didn't last long, either. He was a bigwig. A producer."

"Not the Big Sip?" Joanna said. This was too much of a coincidence.

"Yes," Mary Pat said. "That was him. He had a wandering eye, but he loved me. I know he did. He'd always gone for the blowsy types."

Not like Mary Pat.

"Then he met me. He was at his wit's end with his wife, so possessive, and we both talked about a quiet life where Sip could escape from the craziness in Hollywood and I could keep a big garden. Maybe we'd have children. Does that sound too old-fashioned?"

"Not at all," Joanna said.

"Sometimes people think Hollywood was all about Manhattan cocktails and mink stoles. Maybe it was for some people. At first. Pretty soon the divorces pile on, then the plastic surgery. Sip didn't want it. Neither did I."

"What happened?"

"I still don't know. I can guess, but I don't know for sure. Sip stopped returning my calls. The studio mysteriously dropped me, and the next thing I knew, Bradley was packing our bags." She clutched the coverlet in her fists. "It was his wife, I'm sure. He couldn't say no to her. Bradley and I came home. Mother died soon after. And here I've been ever since."

In that last sentence, Mary Pat had summed up six decades. This grand old house staring unchanged over the river. Now it felt more like a tomb than a home.

"So, you understand. Bradley's death hit me hard. And now Luke…" Her eyes seemed to have grown larger. "Was it poison?"

Now Joanna understood. Mary Pat was alone. And scared. Even on the modest-sized bed, she looked small. Joanna scooted a few inches closer. "Are you worried you might be next?"

Mary Pat grasped the coverlet. Her gaze darted to the doorway then back to Joanna. "I think he's done. He—or she—should be done"—her voice dropped—"killing."

"You mean whoever killed your brother and Luke?"

"Yes. He should be finished, unless…"

"Unless what?"

"Come closer."

Joanna pulled out the desk chair and moved it to the head of the bed. "And who do you mean by 'he'?"

"My brother's memoir had some stories that didn't make certain people look very good."

"He hinted at that when I saw him. You think that's what put him at risk? I'd had the same thought."

"What else could it be?"

"It sounds like you have someone in particular in mind."

"No. Oh, I don't know." She looked perilously close to collapsing into hysteria again.

Joanna poured a glass of water from the bedside carafe and handed it to her. Mary Pat took a dainty sip and set it aside. "Have you talked about this with the police?"

"Not—yet." Her faltering tone told Joanna that "yet" might never come. Mary Pat collapsed against the pillows.

"And these stories. They must have been more than just embarrassing."

She nodded emphatically. "Oh, yes. Some of his stuff could have sent people to jail." She lowered her voice. "For murder."

"So, you've read the memoir," Joanna said.

"No." She looked at her fingertips. "But Bradley told me."

Joanna walked to the window. Trees shaded a stone-paved patio surrounded by parrot-colored canna lilies and other tropical plants Joanna couldn't name. It was quiet on this side, with the freeway's hum insulated by the old house.

She turned to Mary Pat. "It crossed my mind that Luke might have blackmailed people and posed as your brother."

Mary Pat nodded vigorously. "Luke always needed money. Bradley complained about it to me. Luke used to pester him for advances on his pay. Then, once this spring I was setting out a bowl of camellias and I passed him at his computer with Bradley's memoir. He covered the screen when I went by, but I saw he was looking up addresses. What else could it be? He was angry at Bradley for not advancing him more money, so he thought he'd collect it from someone in the memoir."

"Maybe he needed to clear certain passages with people. You know, fact checking. Or see if they were still alive."

"Then why would he hide it from me?"

Joanna couldn't argue with that. "He was planning to leave this morning, you know. His bags are in the entry hall."

Mary Pat's voice dropped. "I'm not surprised. He was packing late last night. I thought he was afraid I'd kick him out now that Bradley is gone, and I tried to reassure him. Now I wonder if he simply wanted to clear out before the police got suspicious."

Joanna returned to the bed and sat. "I guess it doesn't matter now. You'll tell the police about it, of course."

"No. I can't."

"Why not?"

Joanna leaned back and considered Mary Pat. She had been just as privy to the secrets as her brother and Luke. She said she hadn't read the memoir, but why wouldn't she have? She'd been in the same house with it for months. She might have been listening outside the door as Bradley dictated. When it came down to it, how could Mary Pat have avoided knowing what was in the memoir? It hadn't escaped Joanna that Mary Pat had jumped on her theory that Luke's blackmail had killed Bradley Stroden.

Looking in the older woman's eyes, Joanna realized she had already figured this out. Whatever this horrible secret was, Mary Pat knew it. Or could know it. The murderer might want to make sure there would be no further demands for cash and definitely no memoir.

"As for the few stories I've heard, I haven't said a peep all these years," Mary Pat said. "Why would I talk now? Especially given what happened to Bradley?" Her eyes filled with tears.

Joanna wanted to reach out to her, but she still wasn't sure if the sister would welcome it. "Maybe the murderer knows that." She chose her words carefully. "Why did you want to talk with me? I still think it's the police you need to talk to."

Mary Pat sat up. Her eyes were red, but she showed no signs of further tears. "Oh, no. I can't. If they start digging up old crimes, I'm dead."

"Why? Why are you so sure?"

She turned away. "Top drawer of the desk. It came in yesterday's mail."

Joanna slid open the desk drawer. Thinking of Luke downstairs, she hesitated to touch it. Noticing, Mary Pat slowly lowered herself from the bed and pulled out the envelope.

"It's not poisoned. Look." She slipped a letter from the envelope.

The note was printed on plain white paper like that from any office or house, including this one. The envelope had nothing on it but Mary Pat's name. It had been hand delivered. That, or Mary Pat had written it herself. "It stops now or you're next," the note said. Joanna dropped the letter to the nightstand.

"So you see," Mary Pat said, "I can't tell the police."

"You're sure the note refers to blackmail and the memoir?"

"What else could it be?"

"But why me?" Joanna asked. "Why are you telling me? The police can help you so much more. They could put a watch on your house, have someone—"

"That would be my death sentence." Her tone was firm, the firmest Joanna had heard it. "I need your help. I know you've been involved in murder cases before. I read about it in the paper, and I've seen how interested you've been in Luke and Bradley. You didn't really want Bradley's clothes. You wanted to know more. You thought I didn't notice that? And you're not the police."

"I know a good detective you can call. He used to be in homicide, but now—"

"No." Her voice was curt. "You want the Edith Head wardrobe, don't you?"

Joanna looked up. "Well...yes."

"You help me, and the costumes are yours."

Chapter 18

She hadn't agreed to Mary Pat's plea for help. She'd wanted to, but Paul's words rang in her ears. "I'm on your team. Don't forget it."

And yet, she had committed — emotionally, at least.

When she arrived home, an older model Dodge sedan occupied her usual spot in front of the house. She parked across the street and, curious, opened the house's front door. Sitting in the living room were Paul and Gene — and Foster Crisp.

"Foster, what are you doing here?" She dropped her purse on the table by the door and settled next to Paul on the couch. Gemma's tailed thumped hello on the carpet. The bags of clothing in her car from the Stroden house could wait a few minutes.

"I needed to see Gene before deciding to take on your case for certain."

"Wanted to make sure I was really going straight," Gene said.

Joanna had to hand it to him. Some ex-cons when confronted with the policeman who'd put them away years ago might break a sweat. Gene's expression was as crisp as the part in his Brylcreamed hair.

"What did you decide?" The day's drama was not over yet. She kicked off her shoes and tucked her feet under her. Paul put his arm around her and looked ready to say something, but closed his mouth again. She put her hand in his.

"I had to know he wanted my help as much as you did, Joanna," Crisp said. "I'm convinced. So far, at least."

"What's wrong?" Paul whispered.

"I'll tell you later."

Crisp and Gene watched her. Crisp said, "You weren't at the Stroden home today, were you?"

"How did you know?"

"I keep up with police radio. I heard there was another murder up there."

"A what?" Gene said just as Paul swiveled to look at her.

"It's true." Joanna massaged her temples, her fingers trembling. She tucked her hands under her legs.

"You went up there again?" Paul asked.

"It wasn't anything dangerous," she said quickly. "At least, it wasn't supposed to be. Luke, Stroden's secretary, called and asked if I still wanted to buy Stroden's clothes. I closed up the shop and met him." She looked at Paul. "I left you a note. At least, I intended to."

Crisp watched them talk. His gaze left an almost physical imprint. "Luke, huh?" he said. "The possible blackmailer?"

"Blackmail? Start at the beginning," Paul said.

"Hold on. I'll be back in a sec." Gene left the room, his footsteps sounding on the basement stairs. He reappeared with a bottle of Four Roses bourbon and three highball glasses. "I thought we could use a drink."

"I could," Joanna said. "Don't bother with ice."

Crisp accepted a glass, but he kept his eyes on Joanna.

"I saw Luke," Joanna said, "agreed to buy the clothes, and loaded everything into Old Blue. When I went back to get a receipt, he was dead."

"Cyanide again?" Crisp asked.

"He didn't eat anything. Nothing I saw, anyway," Joanna said. "But there was a half-drunk cup of coffee next to him."

"You didn't have the chance to talk to him about anything else?"

"Not for lack of trying."

"Talk to him about what?" Paul asked.

"Just a second, Paul." Then, to Crisp, "I saw the memoir, and a few passages were bookmarked. Plus, Stroden's sister is sure Luke was blackmailing people in Stroden's name."

"Hold on." Paul pulled his arm from behind her and stood. "What are you talking about?"

"It gets worse," Joanna said. "Mary Pat Stroden got a note warning her to 'back off' or she'd be next."

Crisp examined his whiskey glass as if it were a crystal ball. "You don't say. A note?"

"Should we be keeping you?" Joanna asked Crisp. "What's your hourly rate, anyway? I'm not sure we should be chewing up time like this."

"Stop!" Paul's voice was loud enough that Gemma crossed the room and plopped down next to Gene. "Will somebody tell me what's going on?"

"Yes," Joanna said. "Sit down. There's no reason to raise your voice. I was going to, but I didn't expect Crisp would be here, and—"

"Never mind all that. What's this about blackmailing and murder?"

"Let me try, Joanna." Crisp leaned forward and set his tumbler on the coffee table. "When Joanna came to see me about Gene and the Greffulhe jewels, we talked for a few minutes about Stroden's murder. She wanted to know what the homicide team would be doing to follow up." He shot her a glance. "Her interest seemed natural, given that she was there when he died and given her past involvement in murder cases."

"I told you about it," she said.

"Conversation naturally drifted to motive and the idea that Stroden might have been using his memoir as a vehicle for blackmail."

"And that's what got him K.O.ed," Gene finished. "I can see it."

"His sister Mary Pat and secretary Luke also had access to the memoir," Joanna said. Paul had settled again on the couch. "I admit, I did question Luke in a roundabout way. I wanted to know if there was anything in the memoir worth money to anyone. He didn't take my questioning very well."

"Explain," Crisp said.

"He said if I didn't back off, he'd tell Detective Roscoe I murdered Stroden."

"What?" Paul let his hands fall hard on the couch cushions.

Joanna ignored it. "I glanced at the memoir, too."

"Really?" Crisp said. "When did you manage that?"

"While I was waiting for the ambulance to arrive. By chance, I saw it in a drawer."

"This has to stop," Paul said. "I know you're curious, but two people are dead already. It isn't worth the risk."

"I saw just a few paragraphs—"

"It's not just the memoir, Jo. Paul has a good point," Crisp said. "I'll put my antennae up for what's happening at the police bureau, and I'll keep you up to date. But you need to step back."

"I don't know if I can," she replied. Crisp sat, glass in hand, watching her with his usual inscrutable expression. Gene, one hand scratching Gemma's head, was probably happy to find someone else on the receiving end of Crisp's attention for a change. Paul sat stiffly beside her. She wasn't finished. Not yet. There had to be a way out of this.

And then it occurred to her. Maybe there was. She'd heard of ideas crystallizing out of the ether, but she'd never experienced it, until now. She sat straighter. Her idea—it just might work.

"I have two things to tell you," she said. "I'd like you to listen to both of them before you say anything. Agreed?"

"Fine with me," Gene said.

Crisp nodded.

When it became clear that Paul wasn't going to respond, she continued. "When I was at the Stroden mansion today, Mary Pat—Bradley Stroden's sister—said she's sure Luke was using information from the memoir to blackmail people, only he was making it look like Bradley was the culprit. As I said, yesterday she received a note she interprets as warning her not to divulge anything in the memoir, or she'd be killed." Joanna tipped her glass toward Crisp. "Naturally, the same went if she talked to the police about it. She asked me to help her figure out who the murderer is."

"No," Paul said. "Crisp, you tell her. This is crazy."

"Wait," Joanna said. "You promised to listen."

Paul reluctantly settled back. "Okay."

"So, what about this? How about I talk to Mary Pat about making a public statement? She could invite reporters to the Stroden mansion—you know she'll get a full house—and announce that she didn't feel it was appropriate to publish the memoir. Then, in front of everyone, she could toss the memoir into the fire. That would send a public message that there will be no more memoir and no more blackmail."

"Kind of hot for a fire these days," Gene said.

"Or the shredder. Whatever."

"It will be the real memoir," Crisp said.

"Yes. Naturally. The police have a digital copy." Joanna sipped her bourbon. This might actually work, as long as Mary Pat agreed. And why wouldn't she? She'd be removing herself from risk.

"Why do you need to be involved?" Paul asked. "Mary Pat could do this by herself."

Joanna set down her tumbler and raised a finger. "That was the first part. This is the second."

Next to her, she felt Paul's chest rise and fall as he expelled a long breath. "All right."

"Maybe we can use the press conference to solve Gene's situation, too."

Crisp set his now-empty glass on the table, and Gene splashed a bit more inside. "I'd like to hear this."

"Then listen up."

Chapter 19

It was still dark when a clatter in the kitchen awoke Joanna. The clink of dog food in Gemma's bowl and the whine of the coffee grinder were clear signs someone wanted them awake.

"Gene," Joanna grumbled.

Paul stretched and rolled over. "What time is it, anyway?"

"Barely six o'clock."

It was so peaceful in bed. She'd had the best night of sleep in days, now that the Gene situation looked close to being settled. Crisp's opinion that Joanna's plan was sensible and low risk seemed to soothe Paul, and there'd been no tossing and turning during the night on his part, either. Too bad it had to end so soon.

The morning air filtering through the bedroom window was cool, giving no hint of the hot afternoon sure to come. Pepper jumped off the bed and slipped out the door through the shaft of orange light that sliced the dark floor.

"Uncle Gene clearly wants us up," Paul said after a crash of frying pan and spatula.

"It's the press conference. He's antsy. I can't call Mary Pat this early, anyway. You'd think another couple of hours wouldn't be a big deal after all these years."

"He wants to be clean of the past," Paul said. Gene started in on an unseasonal rendition of "Hark the Herald Angels Sing." "Wow, does he ever."

Joanna slipped from bed and reached for a kimono. One hand on the wall to steady herself, she stepped into a pair of green Moroccan slippers with a tassel on each toe. "The baker lady has sure got his number."

In the kitchen, Gene was cracking eggs into a mixing bowl. Joanna wondered if all that family's men were so good in the kitchen. She poured herself a cup of coffee. The whoosh of the shower sounded through the wall between the bathroom and kitchen as Paul started his morning routine.

"You're sure up early," Joanna said.

"Today's the day, right? You're going to see Bradley's sister. You think she'll go for it?"

"We'll see." She twisted her hair up and impaled it with a chopstick. "I thought I'd wait until it was light out to call, though."

Gene left the eggs on the counter and took his coffee mug to the dining room. "It's getting light, see?" Apricot sun stained the sky above the house across the street. He sighed. "I'm sorry. I'm just so ready to have it all behind me." He pulled a folded napkin from the top of the buffet and set it in front of her. "Look."

Joanna peeled back the napkin. Lying on its linen folds were the emerald earrings she'd already seen, now cleaned of stain remover. Next to them lay their dazzling companions, a choker-length necklace and a brooch, both emerald and diamond. She picked up the necklace, and its teardrop emeralds swung freely. The morning light on diamonds spattered the dining room wall with light, but it was the emeralds that caught her eye.

"How many carats in that central emerald? I've eaten Chiclets smaller than that," Joanna said.

"Almost four carats and unusually good quality."

"Why did the woman wear these jewels to a house party in Port-land? You'd think they'd be locked up in a safe and brought out for royal coronations." Yet here they were, on her humble dining room table, next to her grocery list and a set of salt and pepper shakers shaped like Eiffel Towers.

"That was part of this girl's schtick. She had a complete set of fakes. Pretty common. Only she put the fakes in the safe. People would think they were looking at paste, but they were real. 'Best paste you ever saw, huh?' she'd say." Gene got up to refill his coffee cup. "She'd treat them like fakes, too, leaving an earring off while she used the phone."

"How'd you find out she wore the real jewels? I mean, she'd be foolish to tell anyone. Otherwise, why have the set of duplicates at all?"

"You're right. She kept mum about it. When she was sober. Get a grasshopper or three into her, and she'd spill everything."

Looking at Gene now, it took imagination to picture his life as a high-end thief. He was appropriately dapper in a Pink Panther way, sure, but his hair, although slicked into a movie star's wave, was now steel gray and sparse. He was trim enough to wear a tuxedo well, but his daily uniform was jeans with a neat plaid shirt tucked into the waistband.

"Tell me about this woman, the one with the emeralds. What was her name?"

"Aimee. Not spelled the usual way, but like the French word for 'loved.' Aimee Miller."

Joanna leaned back in her chair. "So, how did you pull it off, anyway? Crisp said you had a solid alibi."

Gene took his coffee to the kitchen and busied himself with preparing breakfast. "I don't know what you're talking about."

The bathroom door opened and Paul passed by the doorway wrapped in a bathrobe. If it had been just the both of them, the bathrobe might have been just a towel. Someday, she thought longingly, those mornings would return.

"Okay, you won't tell. Are you willing to admit being at the party?"

He glanced at her, one eyebrow raised, but said nothing.

"Maybe you can tell me what the party was like, at least. You might have heard" —she paused for emphasis—"rumors."

"Oh, sure, I heard about the party." He pulled a brick of cheddar from the refrigerator. "What do you want to know about? The dresses?"

He might be able to give her the lowdown on that, actually. He had a good eye. "You know, the scene. You weren't there. We've established that. But say you were a guest, and you came through the door. What would you have seen?"

"I'll tell you what I heard. It was a cold night. Raining. The party was at the Woodstock mansion up in the West Hills." He grated cheese into a mixing bowl. "This was before the highrises went in, and the views from the porticos stretched out over downtown and the valley to Mount Hood and Mount Saint Helens. That night, the mist covered it all, but you could make out the lights downtown." His hands had slowed their grating of the cheese and his eyes took on a faraway look. "Get him out of Washington and away from the cameras, and Senator Woodstock had a different life." He nodded toward Joanna. "Not for publication, you understand."

"I get it. This was in the seventies, right?"

"Nineteen seventy-three."

Women would have been wearing pastel blouson-topped dresses

and loose-legged pantsuits with pumps. Makeup favored glossy lips. Not her favorite era for couture, but a good one for perfume. She cherished her flacon of old Diorella.

"It was loud," Gene continued. "Good lord. And the crowd was a real mix. Portland's whole underworld was there. Goldilocks—used to be a dancer down at Mary's Club, you knew her, right, Joanna?—was sitting on the baby grand kicking her legs around. Lots of the rich kids showed up." As he talked, in her imagination she saw the crowd, smelled the Harvey Wallbangers, and heard the piano tinkle. "Come to think of it, Bradley Stroden was there, too. Sitting on the couch, watching, nursing his cocktail."

"No kidding. Somehow I'm not surprised."

"He got around, Stroden did. Anyway, the Canadian ambassador was in town, and it turned out that he and the senator shared a taste for the nightlife. The ambassador and his, um, friend, Ms. Miller, were staying in the guesthouse out back. When they came in, the room got quiet-like, just like in the movies. That woman—"

"Aimee," Joanna said.

"She had the whitest skin I've ever seen outside a baby nursery. Pure white but for an adorable sprinkling of freckles right here." Gene touched his nose. "And those emeralds. How anyone could think they were paste—"

"What's for breakfast?" Paul, now dressed in a more rumpled version of his uncle's attire, came in, Gemma at his feet.

"Denver omelet. Going to the job site this morning?"

"Don't stop. Sit down, Paul. You don't want to miss this. Your uncle's in the middle of a good story."

"You're sure you're not bored?"

"Stop joking and get on with it," Joanna said, her coffee cooling at her elbow. "Gene was telling me about the Greffulhe jewel heist."

Paul pulled up a chair. "I'm listening."

"Well, as the night went on, the ambassador's girlfriend tore through the champagne. The other guests were dropping away fast — passing out behind the couch, taking over the guest bedrooms, one even settling into the bathtub. That Aimee could really hold her liquor. You could hear the birds singing, and the sun was coming up behind Mount Hood by the time she was ready to turn in."

"What about the ambassador?" Joanna asked.

"He'd gone to bed long before."

"What did you do next?"

Gene faced them, spatula in hand. "What do you mean, me?"

"Correction," Paul said. "What did the thief do?"

"He was at the party with a friend" — Gene looked knowingly at them — "and hadn't been planning a work night. In fact, he'd spread the word that he was fishing in Idaho. But the product at the party was too good to pass up. I suspect our thief was waiting in the guesthouse, likely under the bed with the ambassador snoring above him. Finally, the girl stumbled in and sat on the edge of the mattress for a long time. The thief was worried she was going to pass out right there."

"Because you needed her to take off the jewels, right?"

He nodded. "Finally, she decided to take a shower. The thief saw her bare feet cross the carpet and the dress fall to the floor. She didn't even bother to hang it up."

"And the jewels?" Joanna said, barely breathing.

"She wore them in the shower. It was starting to get light by then, and the thief was worried about getting out of the guest house before the staff at the main house showed up. Plus, this was an ambassador, at a senator's house, no less. There'd be security staked out at the property's entrances."

Paul lifted the necklace and spread it over the tablecloth. "But the thief prevailed."

"Aimee Miller finally dropped the jewels on the nightstand. Last thing she did before cutting into snores louder than the ambassador's."

Gene set the skillet on the stove. The story of the party was over. Joanna took a last look at the Greffuhle jewels and wrapped them again in the napkin. "I'll call Mary Pat and do what I can to convince her to hold a press conference. In the meantime, I'll find a worthier container for these." She lifted the bundle. "I have a velvet evening clutch that rumor has it used to belong to Lana Turner."

"Thank you. I've been waiting a long time for this day."

Chapter 20

Gambling that Mary Pat was an early riser, Joanna called at nine o'clock. Thanks to Gene, she was long dressed, fed, and ready for the day. Too bad they didn't have chickens to feed and cows to milk. There'd have been plenty of time that morning.

No one answered and no voice mail picked up. She might have dialed the wrong number. Reading the digits carefully from the back of the Tallulah's Closet business card where she'd jotted them a week earlier, she dialed again. Again, no answer.

Worry sparked in her chest. Maybe Mary Pat had been right, and her life had been in danger. Thousands of people in cars clogged the boulevard below her on their way to work, but she was all alone in the big house. It would be far too easy for someone to break in and attack her.

Gene stood in the doorway, watching. "Nothing?"

"Nothing." Thoughtfully, she returned the phone to its cradle. "I'm leaving right now."

"I'll go with you."

"No." Joanna was already at the door. "I'll go alone. If I have to call the police, it's better if you're not there."

Minutes later, Joanna was at the Stroden mansion, feeling as if she were stuck on repeat in a horror movie. She ran up the long stairway to the house's front door, and, gasping for breath, pounded on its carved oak surface. No one answered. She bit off a curse and hurried around a narrow stone path cut into the lawn around the side of the house.

Lilac branches brushed her shoulders as she circled toward the back of the house. Surely she'd find a kitchen door.

She arrived at what should have been the far side of the morning room, just off of the kitchen, and hit a fence. Joanna had worn sensible 1940s wedge-soled sandals and a cotton circle skirt, but this fence was taller than she and built of vertical planks. Nowhere to get a foothold.

She pounded on the gate, constructed flush with the fence, with no visible handle to open it.

"Mary Pat, are you there?" she yelled. The house was so vast that, underlaid with the constant hum of traffic, she wasn't sure she'd be heard even if Mary Pat were a dozen feet away.

She searched the side yard for something to stand on and found a redwood box with a garden hose rolled up in it. She dumped out the hose and dragged the box to the gate. She placed one foot on the box and tested her weight. The box wiggled on the uneven turf. Quickly, she stepped up with her other foot and, thrusting herself forward, grabbed the top of the gate. She couldn't see over, but she could hook the inside of her elbow over the gate's splintery ridge and feel for the latch.

"What are you doing?" said an elderly woman brandishing a poker.

Joanna whirled around to face the voice. She leapt down from the crate. "I'm here to see Mary Pat."

The woman's white hair looked familiar to Joanna. Yes. It was the neighbor who'd spied on her when she first visited, then again on her next visit to Luke. The neighbor wore jeans and a fleece pullover so new they might have just had the tags cut off. It wasn't often you saw pressed jeans. In contrast with her catalog-fresh clothing, a coffee-brown mole by her left eye gave the neighbor the look of a senior Cleopatra.

"What's wrong with the front door?" the neighbor asked.

"I rang the bell, but no one answered."

At last, the woman lowered the poker. "I know you. You've been here before. The day what's-his-name died."

Joanna nodded.

"And the other one. You were here when the other one died, too. Yesterday."

"A terrible coincidence," Joanna said. She willed herself to relax. "Which is why I'm so desperate to see Mary Pat right now. I tried to call, and she didn't answer. I want to make sure she's okay. I'm Joanna, by the way."

"Carol," the neighbor said. She looked right, then left, then at her feet. "Okay," she said finally. "The sister's in the backyard. I saw her from my kitchen." She filled her lungs and tilted her head back and bellowed. "That should do it. Yep. There she is now." The neighbor disappeared through the bushes just as Mary Pat pushed open the garden gate.

Mary Pat must have been gardening—she held a pair of green gloves in one hand and a trowel in the other. "Joanna. Sorry, I didn't hear you."

Joanna followed her through to the backyard. "That's all right. I just met your neighbor, Carol. She saw me at the side gate and wanted to know what I was up to."

"I catch her spying on us all the time, the old busybody, but I haven't actually met her yet."

"She knew you were in the garden. Told me she could see you from her house."

"She just moved in last month. I suppose at some point we should properly introduce ourselves, but Bradley was so busy, and then he was working on his memoir, and we were thinking about visiting L.A., and..." Mary Pat sighed. "Anyway, it's nice to see you."

In contrast to the front yard's conventional treatment of shrubs and rose bushes, the back garden was a tropical jungle. Banana trees and orange canna lilies spread in drifts with a garden shed against the back fence. It was quieter here, too.

"How gorgeous," Joanna said. "I saw it from your bedroom yesterday, but it's even nicer down here."

A smile brightened Mary Pat's face. "Thank you. Bradley let me take over the garden once Mother died. It's the one place I really feel peaceful. It took years to tear out the rhododendrons and azaleas and make something more—" she seemed to search for the right word.

"Exotic?" Joanna offered.

"Yes. If I can't go to the Caribbean, at least I can recreate a bit of it here." She set the gloves and trowel on a glass-topped table next to a bamboo chair. "Would you like coffee? Maybe some iced tea? I've been up for hours, but not everyone is an early bird."

Joanna helped herself to the other bamboo chair. "No, thanks."

Mary Pat stared into the yard, seemingly uncurious about Joanna's arrival. Joanna's mood softened. Stroden's sister had been through a lot and might even still be in shock.

"Listen, Mary Pat, I'm here because I have an idea that should keep you safe. As long as we're right and the murderer's interest is in your brother's memoir, it will work."

Mary Pat turned, and her plaintive, Pickford-like qualities returned. "I hoped you'd think of something. What is it?"

"It sounds a little crazy, but if you consider it, I think you'll find it's a quick and easy way to solve your problem."

"Yes, honey?"

"You'll call reporters and ask them to come to the house this afternoon, that you'll give a public interview."

"What? Today?"

"The sooner the better. For one, the news is still fresh. Plus, the sooner you're out of risk, the better, right?"

She returned her gaze to the garden. "What do I say?"

"You'll start with a statement. Say that you want your brother's memory to be peaceful, and that he had a colorful life, but that you will not be publishing his memoir."

"Oh, I don't—"

Joanna lifted a palm. "I know, but listen. They'll want to talk to you one-on-one, but you'll need to tell them that you only have the strength for one interview, and you only have one message. Then you'll invite them to the house." She leaned forward. "They won't be able to resist the story." She waited for a response, but none came. "Then, right in front of them, you'll burn the memoir."

Mary Pat's jaw dropped. "What?"

"I saw a fireplace in the library. You could burn the memoir on the spot. Photographers will be there, and photos of the burning memoir will be on TV and in the newspapers. If the murderer is paying attention at all, he'll get it. He'll understand you don't plan on telling any stories that your brother might have collected."

Mary Pat's expression calmed again. Joanna waited. Finally, Mary Pat said, "All right. The police took a copy of the memoir from Luke's computer, though, after Bradley died."

"The murderer doesn't know that. Besides, it's not like the police will publish the memoir."

"I guess." She turned again to Joanna, with a pleading voice. "But do I have to? I mean, couldn't you do it instead?"

"No." Joanna drew back. "No, it has to be you. You need to send the message. Plus, it's you the press want to talk to."

"What if they ask personal questions?"

"They will. I guarantee it, but it doesn't mean you have to answer. Just tell them you're overwrought, and go upstairs. The press conference will be over." She clutched her hands in her lap. "I'm sorry. I know it's awful. But if we do this, by tonight you'll be free again."

"Okay."

Joanna took a breath. "There's one more thing."

"Yes?"

"You promised me the Edith Head wardrobe if I helped you, but there's something else I'd like, instead." The words came out with difficulty, but it was the right thing to do. For Paul, she had to clear his uncle. Even if it meant giving up a once-in-a-lifetime vintage haul, the Edith Head costumes.

Mary Pat tilted her head. "What? Not the Limoges, I hope. We're broke, and I need to sell a lot of Bradley's things."

"No, it's not a thing. It's something I'd like you to do. At the press conference."

The lines in Mary Pat's face had deepened even over the past day. She probably hadn't had much sleep. Over the next few minutes, she listened to Joanna's request solemnly.

"What a strange thing life is," Mary Pat said. With both hands on the chair's armrests, she boosted herself to standing. She looked more purposeful now, livelier. "Will you bring in the coffee? We need to plan this press conference. And, if you have a few minutes, I'll show you Bradley's things from Edith. You may not be taking them home, but you'd like a peek, wouldn't you?"

Joanna gathered Mary Pat's coffee mug and saucer and stood. "I have all the time in the world."

Chapter 21

Twice Joanna had been moments from seeing the Edith Head wardrobe—and twice been denied. Mary Pat drew a key from her dress and calmly unlocked the dressing room door. No hitch, no drama.

She cracked the door an inch. "I wish Bradley were here. He knew so much more about it," Mary Pat said. Her hands sank to the pockets in her tunic.

Joanna made out only darkness in the sliver of clothing showing. "But now you're here to carry on his legacy."

"Yes." This seemed to cheer her up enough to pull open the wardrobe doors the rest of the way. "I guess that's true. Strange but true, especially since I'll be destroying his memoir. How much do you know about Bradley's job?"

"With Edith Head?" Joanna asked. "Nothing, really, except that he was her assistant."

The wardrobe wafted the scent of cedar and lavender. A fluff of fabric—cotton batiste, a bit of brocade, and bronze silk chiffon caught her eye.

"His title was Costume Assistant. He didn't do any actual designing for the big stars. But he did design for the supporting players, and he learned to mimic Edith's style of sketching so he could do her drawings. She signed off on them, of course."

"Of course." Joanna clasped her hands behind her back to keep from yanking hangers from the closet.

"Bradley"—Mary Pat paused, looking confused—"What do you think the press will ask me? About the memoir?"

Joanna glanced at the potential glory of the wardrobe, then back to Mary Pat. "Nothing about its substance if you make it clear you haven't read it. You simply talk about what you might have heard over breakfast—say, that your brother expected to have the manuscript done next month, or whatever, and that the publisher was waiting for it, but you're canceling the contract. That's all."

"You really think the murderer will believe it if I burn the pages?"

Mary Pat's tiny figure, anxious expression, and, compared to her brother, lack of guile would make her completely believable to the media. "I wouldn't worry about it. If you say you don't choose to move forward with the memoir, and you make that clear, the press will report it. The murderer will know you're talking to him."

Mary Pat's gaze lost focus, and she stared past Joanna. "So strange…"

"I'd love to see the wardrobe," Joanna nudged.

"Yes. Sorry." Mary Pat turned again to the open wardrobe door. "When *Starlit Wonder* was cancelled, Edith Head was already on her next project. She told Bradley to put the wardrobe into storage so bits and pieces of it could be pulled, should they need it for other productions. So he did."

"But—" Joanna started.

"But he kept the lead actress's wardrobe for himself. Ms. Head gave him permission. It was a real honor. She said the costumes should be preserved as a whole, and she knew Bradley was the person to do it. At least, that's what Bradley told me."

"So, these were costumes Edith Head designed, not your brother."

"Exactly." Mary Pat seemed to be in the moment once again. "The movie was contemporary, so all the pieces are mid-1950s and geared toward a woman in the movie industry."

"Amazing."

At last, Mary Pat stepped aside. A clothing rod ran the wardrobe's length, with a row of drawers along the floor and a shelf up high. "Bradley organized the wardrobe by the script, with the earliest costumes here"—she gestured toward her far left—"traveling along to there." She tapped a finger toward the door. "He said the actress was a bit hippy and her legs weren't great, but she had a sharp jaw and a good bust."

She pulled out a day dress in cocoa-printed polished cotton with a sweetheart neckline and a full skirt.

Joanna stepped forward. "May I?"

Mary Pat shrugged. "Why not? Bradley might have told you not to touch, but I don't see what the big deal is. Not anymore."

Joanna lifted the dress's skirt to see a stiff but thin crinoline. It would have swished around its wearer's calves, giving a sense of motion to distract from thick ankles. She ran her fingers around the neck. Naturally, there wasn't a maker's tag. The craftsmanship was solid, though. The seams and buttonholes were hand finished and the fabric was of good quality. She touched the liquid texture of the fabric's weave.

"This must have been meant for an afternoon scene. What do you know about *Starlit Wonder's* story?" For the moment, she forced herself to focus on Mary Pat instead of the costumes.

"Not much, really. It took place in Hollywood, I know that. The lead—this is her wardrobe—played an actress."

"But the film was never released. I wonder why?"

"No." Mary Pat lifted a patent leather stiletto from the rack lining the wardrobe's floor. "Good grief. I can't believe we ever wore these." She replaced the pump. "It happened from time to time that a movie's production was cut short."

"It must have been a big deal. Think of all the money spent on hiring the crew, paying the actors, building sets—"

"Sewing the costumes," Mary Pat finished. "I know. It was Sip's money to spend. He decided to pull the plug." The older woman's pale blue eyes were gentle.

Joanna turned again to the wardrobe. "What else is there?"

They sifted through the closet's contents, from two suits—maybe the lead character had done secretarial work sometimes?—to two more afternoon dresses and two evening gowns. They were all shades of taupe, some with white collars and cuffs and some not, but all in hues of gray and brown. In taupe, the suit looked business-like, but the silk evening gown raised the color to a whole new level of glamour. With pearls, the dress would have had fashionistas in the audience gasping. She imagined the actress having dark hair and vivid blue eyes.

"So much taupe," Joanna said.

"Not the first color I would have chosen, but it comes off as elegant here, don't you think?"

In the row of taupe, one evening gown stood out. It was gold. This gown sent adrenaline coursing through Joanna's bloodstream, a visceral reaction she felt in the face of intoxicating beauty, and a feeling that struck only once or twice a year.

"I have to see this gown out of the closet," she said. "If you don't mind."

"Fine."

Joanna hung the strapless dress from the door and stood back. It was boned and fitted through the torso, then fell in pleated folds to the floor. A full crinoline fluffed from beneath it as if it had been waiting to be released from the closet and needed only elbow-length gloves and a chauffeured limousine for a nightclub outing.

"Amazing," she repeated, aware that she was starting to sound like one of the Book Bunnies. She wondered what accessories Head would have paired with the dress. A gardenia corsage? Sapphire parure?

"That's about all," Mary Pat said. "Here's the final outfit. Kind of dramatic, huh?"

She pulled from the closet a simple chiffon peignoir in pale gray with lace trim. Just outside of the taupe spectrum. Edith Head must have had a sure eye for color, because this peignoir would not suit just anyone. Joanna reached for the garment, then dropped her hand and gasped. The peignoir was stained with a palm's-width streak of dried blood.

"What—?" she said.

Mary Pat laughed. "It's nothing. Bradley said that in the movie, the lead dies, so they stained the outfit ahead of time. I had the same reaction the first time I saw it. Here's its twin, no blood stains."

"I see." She forced a laugh. "They did a good job." The chiffon was stiff and brick-brown with the fake blood. So, *Starlit Wonder* featured a death, and a bloody one at that.

Mary Pat closed the wardrobe doors before Joanna had had the chance to look at the slippers accompanying the peignoir. "Do you think they'll really come? Today?"

"The press, you mean?" Joanna swallowed a sigh as Mary Pat locked the wardrobe doors. "Yes. If we make the calls, they'll come. Are you ready, though?"

Mary Pat looked at her blankly. "What do you mean? Fix myself up?"

It's not like she needed a fancy wardrobe or a makeup job. In fact, it was better that Mary Pat didn't try to be anyone else. A meek, grief-stricken sister was perfect.

"You're fine just as you are," Joanna said. "All you'll have to do is let them in — I'd think we'll have ten people, maybe a dozen, tops — and read the statement."

"Read it," Mary Pat said.

"Yes, as we discussed. I'll make notes for you. Bradley was writing a memoir, but you won't release it." She had a sudden thought. "You have the manuscript, right?"

"Oh, yes. Definitely."

"Where is it?"

"Don't worry about that. I'll have it ready."

"Fine. Then you say that you have another announcement. Just as we talked about." Joanna watched Mary Pat. Hopefully, she'd keep up this end of the bargain. She could practically taste the joy of having the house to herself and Paul alone again.

"Okay," Mary Pat said.

"Then you'll toss the manuscript into the fire. We'll make a fire before they arrive. We'll invite photographers."

The wardrobe doors were now a flat wall of polished mahogany, locked.

"Okay," Mary Pat said. "Three o'clock?"

Chapter 22

That afternoon, the Stroden mansion's library was full to bursting with people—and hot. Building a fire on an August afternoon might not have been Joanna's brightest idea. The flames danced low behind the screen, and people forced to stand near it were mopping their foreheads.

Not a bad turnout, Joanna thought. Most of the people in the room were local journalists with photographers. Three hoisted video cameras. It hadn't been hard to attract a crowd. Less than an hour on the phone mentioning "double murder" and "old Stroden mansion" had ensured solid attendance. The neighbor's eyes must have popped out of her head when she saw the camera crews arrive.

Joanna sat at the library's edge, near the desk with its copy of Stroden's memoir inside. If only she could pull out the drawer and read it, but she'd never have that chance again. The journalists didn't know that today they'd be getting another newsworthy story, too. One having to do with jewels. One that would wipe Gene's slate clean. Paul and his uncle were on tenterhooks at home.

All the library's windows were open, and Joanna fanned herself with the vintage Japanese fan she kept in her purse. Mary Pat waited in the kitchen.

As planned, Mary Pat entered the library at three o'clock sharp.

She and Joanna had chosen her dress with the goal of emphasizing her age and fragility. Mary Pat's closet was full mostly of practical gardening clothing, but toward the back they'd found a rose-sprigged dress saved for weddings and other Sunday type of events. Joanna had helped her set her hair in her usual long ringlets and had suggested a touch of lipstick so Mary Pat's face would show up better in photographs. Perhaps feeling a throwback to her Hollywood days, Mary Pat had glossed Vaseline on her front teeth. "Better for the camera," she'd said.

The room quieted. Mary Pat entered to snapping cameras and bodies shifting in chairs. Several people fanned themselves with notebooks. She slipped on a pair of reading glasses and read from the statement she and Joanna had prepared earlier, with Crisp's input.

"Hello, everyone, and welcome to my home." She cleared her throat. "As you know, my brother, Bradley Stroden, was murdered earlier this week." She coughed, and cameras flashed.

Joanna wished they'd thought to set up a pitcher of water. Mary Pat's voice was delicate as it was. Facing a room of strangers like gossip-hungry vultures wouldn't be easy at the best of times, and this was not the best of times.

"I invited you here because I have two important messages. When I've finished, I'll open it up to questions. First—" Here, Mary Pat's voice broke again. Thank goodness they'd kept the statement short. "Fifty years ago, my brother found himself in possession of some valuable jewelry. Today, I want to rectify that crime and return the jewelry to its rightful owner."

As Mary Pat spoke, Joanna repeated the words silently with her, urging her on. Once the words were spoken, Gene would be off the hook.

"Excuse me, could you be more specific?" a bald man with a microphone asked.

"You mean he stole it?" a woman asked.

"We'll get to questions later," Mary Pat said. Joanna was impressed. Mary Pat continued. "These jewels, known as the Greffulhe emeralds, disappeared at a party Bradley attended at Senator Woodstock's house. I don't know how he came to have them, but Bradley never could resist beauty. As you can see, he kept the jewels all these years and didn't want to profit from them."

Joanna had thought that last bit was inspired. Gene had contributed it.

"And I'm certain he would not rest easy unless he knew they were returned."

Mary Pat stood still a moment. Joanna scooted to the edge of her seat. This was where Mary Pat was supposed to reach to the mantel and bring down the box with the jewels. Joanna caught her gaze and nodded toward the mantel.

"Oh, yes," Mary Pat said. "Here they are."

As she reached for the box, a sudden thought crossed Joanna's mind. What if the box were empty? That morning, Joanna had swaddled the jewels in a velvet clutch, then slipped it into her bag — a black alligator Lucile of Paris she brought out for important occasions. She'd seen Mary Pat transfer the jewels to the box, but hadn't been with her every minute after that.

Mary Pat opened the cloisonné box. The sun had passed over this part of the house, and in the room's dim light, they looked like a jumble of costume jewelry. But here they were, with no mention of Gene.

Joanna nearly melted with relief. It had worked. Her plan had worked. At least, so far.

One reporter, scrolling through her phone, asked, "Did Mr. Stroden know Senator Woodstock?"

Joanna tensed, but she needn't have worried. Mary Pat ignored the reporter and returned to her statement. "That was the first thing. The second item I want to address is my brother's memoir. My brother spent several years in Hollywood as a costume assistant. Along the way, he was privy to compromising stories about celebrities." She crossed to the desk and opened a drawer. She placed a fat file folder of pages on the desktop. "For the past year, he'd been compiling those stories in a memoir."

Something was different about the memoir, Joanna noted. The file folder. This one was manila. The one Joanna had seen had been blue. Mary Pat must have swapped them out.

"As the inheritor of my brother's papers, I'm choosing to destroy the memoir." She slowed down and enunciated her words. "I'm destroying it completely. No one shall see it. I don't feel it's right that people — even people no longer with us — should be humiliated and their relatives hurt by things they did decades ago."

As the reporters shouted questions, Mary Pat pulled aside the fire screen and lifted the file folder. She turned toward the room and cameras flashed.

"Now, I'll burn it." With a dramatic flourish worthy of Margay, Mary Pat opened the folder and dumped its contents onto the flames.

The fire caught the pages and blackened their edges. Flames grew paler and leapt higher.

Joanna turned away. That was it. They'd done it. Bradley Stroden's secrets were going up the flue. The murderer would know his transgressions would remain under wraps, and the jewels would soon be on their way home. Mary Pat could sleep well tonight. Gene could pack his bags. Yet she felt a twinge of regret that it all ended here.

"Wait!" a reporter in a white suit shouted.

A tall man at her shoulder swung his camera toward the fireplace. Joanna jumped to her feet.

"The memoir," the reporter said, "It's all blank pages."

Chapter 23

The room broke into shouts and motion.

"Where is the memoir?" an elegant African American reporter asked. Joanna had no idea the reporter was so tall in person.

"It's a stunt," another reporter said.

All the while, cameras flashed and videos ran. Mary Pat stood, stupefied, next to the now-roaring fire. Bits of paper edged in orange cinders danced in the chimney.

"I don't understand," she kept saying. "I don't get it. The memoir was there this morning."

Joanna raised her hands. "Quiet, everyone. Ms. Stroden, do you have further comments?"

Mary Pat shook her head, dazed. Joanna led her from the fire to the window.

"Sit down," she said, still regretting the lack of water pitcher.

"I don't understand. The memoir—"

"I know. Take a couple of deep breaths." Joanna could use a few deep breaths herself. Now, instead of broadcasting Mary Pat's statement and the memoir's destruction, they'd report that the memoir was stolen. At least Gene was off the hook for the emeralds. Once she got them to the police, that is.

Joanna spent the next half hour shepherding reporters from the house and promising a follow-up if any new information arose. When, at last, the room was empty, Joanna pulled up a chair. "Mary Pat? What happened?"

Mary Pat burst into tears. Joanna was learning she was an easy crier. "I don't know. I tell you, the memoir was there. I checked this morning."

"You know what this means, right? It means the media will be reporting that someone stole the memoir." Mary Pat began to wail again, and Joanna placed a hand on her arm. "Of course, the murderer might have been the one who stole it. In that case, we're in the clear."

"Do you think so?" Mary Pat raised a handkerchief to her nose.

"I'm not sure who else would have wanted it. What puzzles me is how it was stolen. You said the memoir was here this morning. Did you look inside the folder?"

Mary Pat slumped against the window. "No. I saw it in the drawer Bradley always kept his pages in, and I didn't have any reason to think someone might have taken it."

So, the memoir might have been stolen anytime between yesterday afternoon, when Joanna saw it, and today. About twenty-four hours. "Has anyone except me visited you?" It had to have been someone who'd had enough time to rifle drawers, too. Or someone who'd known of Stroden's habit of keeping the manuscript in the library.

"The police were here."

"Besides them. Did any friends visit? Did you call anyone to come over and comfort you?"

"No. I wanted to be alone."

It was too late to fingerprint the desk now. A dozen reporters had had their hands on it. A smart thief would have worn gloves, anyway.

"I'm sorry, Mary Pat. Let's assume the murderer got the memoir and knows it's not a threat anymore. Really, that's the most likely scenario."

"I know." Mary Pat twisted the handkerchief in her fingers. "It's just that I feel so bad for you."

"For me?" Joanna sat again.

"I —" Mary Pat's voice petered out.

"You what?"

"I just…well, I read the memoir. There. I said it." Joanna opened her mouth to speak, but Mary Pat continued. "I couldn't help it. Bradley was so secretive, and I couldn't figure out why. I stole the key a month ago or so, then snuck down in the middle of the night to read it."

Here was the one person besides Luke who knew what was in the memoir. The one person who might know if it really was the cause of Stroden's and Luke's deaths. "Was it, well, was it all that bad?"

"Stylistically, yes. Bradley was a wonderful designer, but he needed an editor."

"You know what I mean. Was anything there someone would kill for?"

"I need something cool to drink," Mary Pat said. "It's too hot in here. Let's go to the kitchen."

Joanna followed her through the entry hall, now quiet, then through the morning room to the kitchen. As formal as the front rooms were, the kitchen was large, but comfortable, almost like a sitting room, with ruffled gingham curtains and a vase of zinnias — thankfully, not violets — on the linoleum-topped table.

Mary Pat pulled a pitcher from the refrigerator. "Would you like some iced tea?"

Remembering Luke's coffee and Bradley Stroden's pastilles, Joanna shook her head. "A glass of tap water would be nice, though."

When they were finally settled at the table, Mary Pat gulped from her iced tea, then faced Joanna. "I'll just come out with it. I read the memoir. It talked about the Greffulhe emeralds. Bradley was clear that your husband's uncle stole them. He was there. That was just like Bradley. If he thought something was going to happen, he stuck around until it did." She toyed with the hem of her skirt. "He said Gene broke in here, too."

Damn, damn, damn, Joanna thought. And damn. "So, whoever has the manuscript knows you weren't telling the truth back there."

She nodded.

"Does anyone else have a copy of the memoir, besides the police?"

Mary Pat shook her head. "No. At least, I don't think so."

She'd have to go home, report this to Gene, Paul, and Foster Crisp. True, the jewels would soon be on their way to their owner. Plus, the statue of limitations on the theft was over. But linking the heist to Gene would cloud his reputation for good. He wouldn't rest easy—or leave their basement—until he felt his name was clear and he'd rectified this crime. She hadn't made things better. She'd worsened them. She heaved a sigh that rustled the flowers on the table.

"I'd hoped it would end today," Joanna said.

"I know," Mary Pat said.

"What else was in the memoir? Why does the murderer want it so badly?" Joanna considered that Mary Pat herself would have been able to steal the memoir very easily. Sure, she looked innocent, but she was an actress. If Mary Pat wanted to turn a buck, what better way than to pretend innocence and sell the memoir for even bigger money later?

"There was a lot of this and that about affairs and a particular actor who cross-dressed. But he's dead," she added quickly.

"What about *Starlit Wonder*?" Joanna said and pushed her glass out of the way. "What did he say about that?"

She shook her head. "I looked for it, but I didn't see anything. Really."

Joanna believed her. Mary Pat would have rifled through the pages looking for anything about her ex-lover, the film's producer. "You saw the draft a month ago, you said? Maybe your brother hadn't dictated that part yet."

"Probably."

Joanna focused on keeping her voice gentle. "Did you know anything about the film? Surely your brother must have mentioned something over the years."

"Nothing, really."

"It's important, Mary Pat. Anything you remember about *Starlit Wonder* is important. Please, think."

"Well, Bradley told me one thing, but it might not be true, so I hate to repeat it."

"What was it? At this point, even rumors are worth considering." Joanna thought of the Head-designed costumes upstairs. Considering the bloodied negligee, death was definitely part of the script. Was murder?

"He said the movie was about a real life story. That's why it was pulled."

*
**

Preoccupied with the vanished memoir, Joanna descended the front steps slowly. The Greffulhe jewels were packed in her alligator bag, and she didn't want any risk of taking a tumble, then having to wrestle for emeralds in the gutter with the low-rent neighbors.

She halted halfway down. Leaning against Old Blue was Detective Roscoe, and he didn't look happy. Joanna glanced at the neighbor's house, and, once again, the curtains rustled. She'd no doubt had a heyday with the reporters coming and going. Someone should get that woman a TV set or jumbo book of crossword puzzles.

"What was that about?" Roscoe said, raising his chin toward the Stroden mansion.

Joanna returned her keys to her purse. "If you don't know, why are you here?"

Roscoe wore a creased panama hat against the sun with dirt stains where he'd pulled it by the brim. He took it off and fanned himself. "A little cranky, are we? Leave your car here. We'll come back for it later." He crossed the street to a gray sedan. "Come on."

"Where are we going?"

"To the station. It's cooler there, and quieter." He gestured toward the house next door. "And the neighbor won't be watching."

Joanna hesitated only a moment before getting in the passenger side. She supposed it was inevitable. And he had noticed Carol. "Have you talked to her? The neighbor? She seems to keep a close eye on the Stroden household."

"Yeah, of course we did. Not that it's any of your business. Not that any of this is your business."

She waited, but he didn't offer more. "I suppose you want to know why Mary Pat Stroden called a press conference."

"Save it for the office."

He didn't speak again until they arrived. It was a quick drive over the Ross Island Bridge, up the boulevard bordering the river, then a

few blocks to the central police station. Roscoe flashed his ID at the
security guard, and they took the elevator to his floor. He had one of
the windowless offices clustered in the center. He flicked on the lights.

"Take a seat. Thirsty? It's hot out."

"No, thank you." She sat primly. Answer what you're asked, she
thought. No more. Especially if it involves Uncle Gene.

"Okay, shoot," the detective said.

"What?"

"Tell me what went on back there. For real. I heard you held a
press conference."

"What do you want to know? I mean, specifically?"

"I want to know what was going on back there."

Joanna dropped her purse to the floor. Fine. "You want to know
the truth? Here's the truth. Mary Pat was worried that the person
who killed her brother and Luke would kill her, too." She laid her
palms on his desk and leaned forward. "Have you discovered what
killed Luke yet?"

"Cyanide. In the coffee."

"Cyanide." Joanna would fast for days before she'd take so much
as a glass of water in that house.

Despite Roscoe's relaxed posture—leaning back, his hands behind
his head—his gaze was laser sharp. "Why was Mary Pat so worried?"

"Because of Bradley's memoir. She got an anonymous note telling
her to back off. She figured the killer would think she'd read the
memoir, too, and was planning to publish it or blackmail him. She
saw herself as his next victim."

"Had she?"

"Read it?"

"Yes. Did she read her brother's memoir?"

Joanna sighed. "She did. Well, she skimmed it, anyway. She was light on specifics."

"And why haven't I seen this anonymous note?"

"I told her she should give it to you, but she refused. She said the murderer would know if she called you." Joanna moved to the edge of her chair. "You have the memoir, right? You'd know if there was something in it worth killing over."

"We've got it. Haven't read it yet. Just a moment." He picked up the phone. "Nora? Yeah. Could you get me a flash drive from the evidence file on the Stroden case? Thanks." He replaced the receiver. "Now, why a press conference? Keep going."

"As I said, Mary Pat was afraid she'd be killed, so I suggested she publicly burn the memoir. Do it in front of witnesses. After all, you already have a copy," Joanna quickly added. "So, it's not as if we were destroying evidence."

Roscoe relaxed back into his hands-behind-his-head posture, gaze steady. "Go on."

"That way, the murderer would see—get the message—that Mary Pat didn't intend to publish it. The murderer's secrets would be kept. It's a big enough story to interest the press. We called a few people, and they came. And then, well…"

"Yes?"

"The memoir had disappeared. Completely." So far, nothing about the Greffulhe jewels. Once he read the memoir, though, all bets were off.

Roscoe rocked his chair forward and leaned on the desk. "The sister didn't just misplace it?"

"No. She said she'd put it in the desk, but someone had replaced it with blank pages. It was important to her. Besides, she'd seen it just the day before." Joanna's mouth felt dry. She wished she'd taken that glass of water after all.

"And that's it? There wasn't, say, a mention of emeralds?"

Joanna flash-froze a smile she hoped didn't look like a grimace. "Emeralds?"

"Roscoe?" A brunette with buzz-cut hair popped her head in the door. "Here's the evidence you wanted."

He rose to take a plastic bag from her, but he kept his eyes on Joanna. "Thanks, Nora. Now, you were saying?"

Joanna unclipped her purse to the scent of leather and her handkerchief dipped in vintage Miss Dior. She placed the velvet-wrapped bundle on the desk. Roscoe pulled it toward him and unsnapped the evening bag's flap.

"Holy Christ." He rolled an earring in his palm. "Anything you want to tell me about them?"

For a split second she entertained the fantasy of saying, "Not really," and wishing him a good afternoon. "They're called the Greffulhe jewels," she said weakly, "and they're stolen. Maybe you could help get them to their owner? It's all in the memoir."

If Roscoe questioned Mary Pat, he'd discover in an instant that Joanna had asked her to lie about the Greffulhe jewels. And if what Mary Pat had said was true about the heist being in the memoir, Gene would be called out as the thief. She had nothing left to hide, but nothing would convince her to rat out Gene directly.

"Then let's have a look." Detective Roscoe slipped Stroden's flash drive — shaped like a red stiletto, she noticed — into his computer. Joanna leaned forward, but the screen was out of view.

"No password." Roscoe shook his head. "If this memoir was such a hot item, you'd think he'd at least password-protect it."

"According to his secretary, Stroden wasn't very tech savvy. He didn't even use a computer—Luke took dictation."

Roscoe clicked the mouse. The air from a ceiling vent rustled his gray frizz. "And there's the file. Double-click here…"

Joanna bit her lip. This was it. Roscoe wouldn't read the whole thing in front of her. That was ridiculous. But maybe she'd learn what the murders were all about. Maybe she'd even get a hint of who'd done them. On the other hand, this could be the end of it for Gene.

His eyes drew together. "Hmm."

"What is it?" She scooted forward as far as the desk between them would allow. "It's not blank, is it?" To protect himself, Luke might have handed over a fake flash drive. She wouldn't have put it past him.

Roscoe scrolled through the pages. "It's not blank. There are a few files here." He clicked the mouse a few more times, then nudged it aside.

"But something's wrong," Joanna said.

He squinted at the screen, then yanked the flash drive out of the computer. "They're empty. Someone's erased every file."

Joanna could only stare. It was inevitable, she realized. Luke would not let the police have anything that might lead to uncovering his blackmail.

Roscoe pushed back his chair. "I'll have someone take you back to your car."

She picked up her purse, now lighter without its freight of diamonds and emeralds. "Not you?"

"I've got to get to work. I want that note to Mary Pat. And if the memoir exists anywhere in the Stroden house, I'll find it."

Chapter 24

The next morning, Joanna was once again at Portland's Central Library when its doors opened. This time, she walked past the information desk, waving at its occupant, to the area where middle schoolers prepared for the Story Challenge. She sat at a broad oak table where she had a view of the door.

As she waited, she thought about her next steps. She hadn't heard anything from Detective Roscoe—a good sign as far as Gene was concerned. Either Roscoe hadn't yet found another copy of the memoir, or he wasn't focusing on the jewel theft aspect. While Roscoe pursued the memoir, she planned to see what headway she could make in finding *Starlit Wonder*.

Half an hour later, Mindy and the two other Book Bunnies trudged in and dumped their backpacks on chairs.

Joanna rose to meet them. Mindy wore the charm bracelet she'd given her. "Hi, girls. Want to make a few bucks?"

Pearl's gaze sharpened. "How?"

"Remember when I first met you, how I wanted to find a movie script? I need some fresh ideas about how to get it."

Mindy glanced at Pearl and Lucy. "Why us?"

"You did such a great job of tracking down Callie Rampton, and you seem to be good researchers."

"And you're clueless about computers," Pearl said.

Joanna ignored her. "I thought maybe you'd be interested in earning a little money over summer vacation. It has to be better than babysitting." Did girls even babysit anymore? She had no idea.

The other girls folded their arms, but Mindy asked, "What do you know?"

Joanna took a seat at the table they'd chosen. "You already know some of this. The movie's called *Starlit Wonder*. It was filmed in 1955, but never released. Extra cash if you can find the film."

"What else?" Mindy said.

Joanna drew an index card from her bag. "One of the actresses—not the lead—is Callie Rampton. The producer's name was David Sipriano. Oh, and I don't know if it will help, but the costumes were by Edith Head."

The shy girl, Lucy, lifted her head. "Know anything about the story?" Her voice was as light and clear as a temple bell.

"Not much. It takes place in Hollywood, and the lead actress dies."

"Really?" Pearl said. "That's all?"

"That's why I want the script. To find out more about it," Joanna said.

"We could try the scriptwriter's personal papers," said Mindy. She'd already popped open her laptop. "A lot of screenwriters left their papers to UCLA. That might be a good place to start, that is, if they're cross-indexed by script titles. What's the writer's name?"

"I'm afraid I don't know that, either. How did you find out about the UCLA collection?" Joanna asked.

"You said we were good at research," Pearl pointed out.

Mindy tapped at the keyboard. "Peter Blackburn."

"What?" Joanna said.

"Peter Blackburn wrote *Starlit Wonder*, and his papers are at UCLA.

Like I thought."

This might actually be easier than she'd anticipated. "Can I order the script somehow?"

"Don't know. It might not even exist anymore." She looked over the laptop's screen. "Anyway, you said you'd pay, right?"

"You get me the script, and you get a hundred dollars, or two hundred in trade at my shop. Plus costs for copying or overnight delivery or whatever it takes to get it to me right away." She leaned forward. "Interested?"

All three of the girls looked alert. Which one would own up to wanting the job?

"I think we should do it. I want to buy some crutches," Lucy said, finally.

"Are you all right?" From what Joanna could tell, Lucy's legs were just fine.

"She's all right," Mindy said. "She just thinks crutches are cool."

"Great." Joanna stood. "Then it's settled."

"I guess we can work on it now," Pearl said, letting a hank of black hair fall in front of her eyes. Mindy's hands went to the keyboard again.

Joanna picked up her purse and stood. "I'm glad you're taking it on. I don't want to take you away from your studying, though. What about the Story Challenge?"

Pearl snorted. "Like we're going to win that, anyway."

⁎⁎

Callie Rampton met Joanna at the door of Stamp Gurlz. "You decided to come back for a stamp of your shop's address, didn't you?"

Joanna hadn't ginned up subterfuge for her visit. She'd been planning simply to ask Callie to talk some more about *Starlit Wonder*. But maybe the stamp idea wasn't so bad. Apple seemed to be into them.

"Yes, and something else, too."

"Well, come in. I was just cutting out some stamps. You don't mind if I work while we talk, do you?"

Joanna followed Callie into the tiny living room-slash-showroom. A stack of boxes partially blocked the door.

"Sorry about that," Callie said. "Big order for a scrapbooking convention in Ohio. Have a seat."

Joanna took the other side of the couch—Callie's side being obvious by its half-drunk bottle of cola, stacks of wooden blocks, and sheets of rubber. The television droned about tips for gardening without pesticides. Callie clicked it off.

"So, what are you thinking for your stamp? You do a simple address, maybe highlight the name of the boutique in a larger font." Callie's focus wavered as she thought. "Maybe with an opera-length glove underlining the boutique's name?"

"I like that," Joanna said. "Could you do a larger stamp for bags?"

"Do it all the time. You'll need ink pads. Does the shop have a color scheme?"

"No. Not really." Tallulah's Closet was a magpie's collection of things she liked, colors and patterns included.

"Got to think about branding, you know." Callie picked up a pair of scissors and, keeping the scissors stationary, turned the rubber as she cut. "Don't you find cutting things out relaxing? It's so meditative. I could do it all day."

"Scissors aren't my thing, but I know what you mean. For me, it's flipping through the racks at thrift stores."

Thrift stores didn't yield much these days, unfortunately. As Portland had grown, drawing hipsters from among the fifty states like a magnet draws straight pins, Goodwill's booty had declined significantly. Just ten years ago, Joanna could hit a suburban thrift store and be sure of an armload of Pendleton skirts, Scottish cashmere, and a few good coats. Maybe even some Henry Waters Shoes of Consequence pumps. Today, she was lucky to find a Jantzen blouse. Every once in a while, though, she'd hit the jackpot, like last week when she'd stumbled on a late 1960s Gucci convertible bag. Unbuckle the bag's outer blue leather sheath, and the inside made a satin evening clutch. But the looking alone was worth it. She'd done some of her best thinking at thrift stores.

"Did you hear that Bradley Stroden's secretary died?" Joanna asked.

Callie set her project on the coffee table to give Joanna her full attention. "No. How did I miss that? Was the secretary murdered like Bradley was?"

Joanna nodded. "Sounds like it was cyanide, too. In his coffee." Interesting that Callie jumped straight to murder.

Callie's eyes widened. "I can't believe it. It's like on TV. I just hope this one won't be on *Unsolved Mysteries*. Although Bradley might have enjoyed the drama." She wrinkled her nose. "Or not. Considering." She pulled an order sheet from the jumble of rubber stamp materials on the table.

"I didn't come here just for a rubber stamp," Joanna said. "I wanted to ask you about *Starlit Wonder*. Because of the murders."

"What makes you think their deaths have anything to do with *Starlit Wonder*? That movie's at least sixty years old, and it never even came out. Like I told you last time, it was no big deal."

"It was something Mr. Stroden hinted at before he died."

Callie raised an eyebrow. "Really? Why aren't the police following up on it, then? No one has called me about it."

"Not yet." Joanna smoothed her skirt over her knees. "I was there when the secretary died, too, and I want to make sure they consider every angle."

The older woman faced Joanna head-on. "I shouldn't have let you in the door."

Joanna froze. "Why's that?"

Then she smiled. "You'd better hope I don't keel over, too."

Joanna laughed in relief. "You're right. But, *Starlit Wonder*. You were on the set." She remembered the Edith Head costumes, the row of stone hues in every texture. And that amazing gold evening gown. "Maybe you don't remember a lot of controversy, but why not tell me about the story?"

"Hmm," she said. "What do you want to know?"

"Mary Pat said she'd heard her brother mention something once about the movie." She looked sideways at Callie. "That *Starlit Wonder* was based on a real life incident."

"She said that, huh?"

Joanna nodded.

Callie fidgeted with her scissors, then set them aside. "Okay. I'll tell you what I know." She settled back into the couch and tucked her legs under her in a motion that she might have done since she was a teenager. "There was talk. Listen—"

The doorbell interrupted them. Callie opened the door to the brown-uniformed deliveryman. "Nothing for you today, but I saw your sign for a pickup," he said.

"Hello, Arnie. It's the stack of boxes to your left. You might need to bring in the hand truck for this one."

At last, someone seemed able to tell Joanna about *Starlit Wonder*. So much mystery surrounded the film. If the Book Bunnies couldn't get her the script, she'd still have Callie's summary. She hoped.

Once the boxes were wheeled out to the delivery truck, Callie returned to the couch. "Where were we?"

"*Starlit Wonder*."

"Yes. Well, *Starlit Wonder* was a noir movie. Kind of dark, you see. It had to do with Hollywood and a murdered starlet."

"Yes?" Joanna barely breathed.

"I don't remember the details—it's been a few years, you know—but the gist was that a movie producer had an affair with an actress, and when she threatened to tell his wife, he knocked off the mistress."

"If the movie reflected real life, then the actress—the real one, not the actress who played the actress in the film—was murdered."

Callie nodded. "I follow you."

"So, who decided to stage the movie? Who wanted to get revenge on the producer? Did the actress have a steady boyfriend?"

"No, it was her brother." Callie's voice gained earnestness. "The grapevine had it that the actress's brother wanted revenge on the producer. He was a screenwriter. He wrote *Starlit Wonder*."

"Then why did the producer ever agree to fund the movie? Sipriano would have known the movie's plot. He could hardly have been successful if he put his name on films he didn't know anything about."

Sunlight gleamed from the lenses of Callie's Edith Head glasses, hiding her eyes. "I heard it from Howard. He's a Portland boy who was on the set as crew. He said that after the screenwriter's sister died, the screenwriter confronted Sip. Sip denied harming his sister. Sip must have felt bad for him, though, because he promised to bankroll his next screenplay."

"Felt bad or guilty," Joanna said.

Callie shrugged. "Could be."

"So," Joanna continued, "the movie was never released, because once the producer discovered what it was about, he didn't want the story to go public. It implicated him." If this were true, the murder—the real one—would have been in the papers. She'd find it.

"That's what they said. No one could prove anything, though."

"What do you think?"

Callie picked up her scissors and dug them again into the sheet of black rubber. "It was a long time ago. I barely remember."

"You seem to remember quite a bit, actually. Maybe you just don't want to talk about it."

Callie let out a long breath. "Like I said, the Big Sip had a repu-tation for having an active casting couch. Look, I don't know. He had lots of kids, seemed dedicated to his family. But he had a libido and the opportunity to indulge it whenever he wanted. That was Hollywood in those days. These days, too, probably. Maybe he had an affair with the actress. Did he murder her? I doubt it. He sure didn't go to prison for any murder."

Joanna looked at her a long minute. If Callie's current pulchritude were a hint of her looks fifty years ago, she would have earned a lot of wolf whistles. "Mary Pat said she'd had an affair with Sip."

"Poor Bradley," Callie said. "We were tight friends at one point, then…" Her voice trailed off. She seemed to be thinking of some-thing in particular. She shook her head. "Yeah, Sip and Mary Pat had something going on. It was after the affair that Bradley took Mary Pat back to Portland. She'd gone a bit batty and needed the stability." Callie focused on her scissors. "At least, that's what Bradley told me."

Joanna considered this news. If *Starlit Wonder* mirrored a producer killing an actress, it would be the producer who'd want to keep Stroden's memoir from being published. He'd be the man blackmailed, and the man who'd kill to cover up an earlier murder. The producer would have to be fairly old now, but it didn't take youth to poison a man. She was on to something, she knew it. She needed to get to a phone.

"So, David Sipriano. The producer. Is he still in Hollywood?"

"Oh, no," Callie said. "He's been dead for years."

Chapter 25

The next morning, Joanna found Gene in the kitchen nursing a cup of coffee. To beat the heat, Paul had left for work early. So far, Gene had shown no sign of moving. No packing, no talking about neighborhoods, nothing.

"Coffee?" Gene asked. "I set out the mug you like. Lovely dress, by the way."

"You like it?"

"Nineteen-forties, right?" Gene said. "Peplum waist and bell sleeves to the elbow. An unusual touch for that era. Paul said you were going out last night. Have fun?"

They'd had fun all right. It had been months since they'd been able to plan a date night knowing Gene wouldn't be home. After tossing around grand ideas ranging from five-star restaurants to watching *His Girl Friday* at the Hollywood Theatre, they opted for listening to the organist at the Oaks Park skating rink and following it up with chicken and jojos at the Reel M Inn. She hadn't laughed so hard in a long time. Best of all, they hadn't talked about the Stroden case.

"We did. I was surprised to find you home, though. I thought you'd planned to be away."

"Oh, you know."

She took her cup to the table. "Gene, out with it."

He fidgeted with a coffee spoon. He had the same graceful fingers and strong hands Paul did. "What?"

"You've been like this the past few days, walking on eggshells."

He sighed. "I tried to tell Paul yesterday, but we got into sharpening the lathe, and the conversation kind of lost its thread."

"You should be in a pretty sweet spot now," Joanna said. "Your name is clear, you're out of prison, and you have a girlfriend who makes a mean pie." So far, no memoir had appeared to spoil it, either.

His face fell. "About that…"

"You broke up?"

"She's an honest woman," he said earnestly.

"You're honest, too, now, right?"

He nodded.

"Then what's the problem?"

"Well, Mary Pat Stroden said her brother had the jewels all these years."

"And?" This morning's coffee was especially delicious. If Gene and his sweetheart decided to open a cafe, they had a winning combination.

"That's just it. It isn't honest, and Melba knows it."

Joanna set down her cup. "What do you mean?"

"I know you were trying to make the situation easy for me, and I wouldn't blame you if you wanted your house back to yourself. I'm ready to get on with my life, too. But Melba says the situation with the Greffulhe jewels won't be over until I come clean about it."

This deserved a second cup. "Want more coffee?" Joanna asked. He shook his head, and, thinking hard, she refilled her mug, topping it off with cream. "Who is this Melba, anyway?"

"Oh, she's marvelous." The set of Gene's expression hadn't changed, yet a pink glow seemed to suffuse him. "I never thought I'd fall in love. I figured I was a loner for good. And that was fine. Do I sound like an idiot?"

Joanna smiled. "Not at all. I know the feeling."

"At my age, even." He shifted his gaze toward the dining room window and flipped the silver coffee spoon between his fingers. "Go figure. Melba—that's her name—was our getaway driver's little sister. I've known her for years."

"But she was never part of the life?"

"No. Absolutely not. She worked in a family restaurant out by the docks and picked up the pastry chef part of the job, then opened her own catering business. Strictly legit."

"Then how does she know Bradley Stroden didn't steal the emeralds after all?"

"Melba's a family girl, too, you know. Her brother never had any secrets from her."

"And her brother knew all about the heist."

"Oh, yes. I'm afraid it's almost legendary in my circle."

"I see your problem." The coffee roused Joanna's appetite even while his news dampened it. "So, the fact that the jewels are going back to their owners isn't enough for her. What does she want? Does she expect you to find the heirs, invite them over for a drink, and admit to having stolen the jewels? What would that change?"

"She says although I might not still be a thief, I'm not being truthful, and that not telling the truth is a kind of stealing, too."

That sounded like a stretch to Joanna, but she was listening. "Go on."

"Plus, if the police find out I stole the jewels, I could get in trouble with my parole officer."

"But you stole them so long ago. It doesn't count anymore, does it?"

"Stealing them doesn't count. Keeping stolen property does."

Gene was a handsome man—fit, handy, and knew how to flat-ter the ladies. He could find another girlfriend. "Are you sure she's worth it?"

"I'm sure. I'm positive. Honey, I've never felt this way in my life. But she says she won't be with someone who isn't truthful."

"What exactly does she want you to do?"

He set down the coffee spoon and pushed it away. "She wants me to apologize. To Aimee Miller."

The next afternoon, Joanna was at Tallulah's Closet, dusting the top of the jewelry display, when Mindy entered, a package under her arm. Thunder rumbled in the distance, and the air was thickening. Mindy's ever-present coat might actually come in handy today.

"You're here. So soon," Joanna said.

"You said you wanted it right away."

Joanna took the bundle from her. "Are you kidding? I've been counting the minutes. Did Kelsey at the library get you those arti-cles, too?"

"Yep. Plus, we found the script right after you left and had them overnight it." As the girl talked, her gaze roamed the store. "We paid extra for the fastest delivery. It sounded like you wouldn't care."

"No, I'm glad you did." She pressed her hands on the weighty package. Inside might well be the key to Bradley and Luke's murders.

"UCLA said they had the film, too."

Joanna's head shot up. "Can we get it?"

"Nope."

"They won't lend it?" For a split second, she wondered what it would take to fly to Los Angeles that afternoon.

"They'd lend it — if they had it. They said somebody borrowed it years ago and never brought it back. There was even a note in the file that they'd tried to find the person who checked it out, but it turned out to be a fake name."

It was getting better and better. Or worse and worse, depending on your perspective. The shop wouldn't close for another four hours, but maybe Joanna could squeeze in reading between customers. "Thank you so much. I couldn't have done this without you."

"I know," Mindy said.

"So." Joanna set the wrapped script on the tiki bar. "What will it be? Cash or trade?"

Mindy was caressing the sleeve of a wool crepe evening jacket. "I don't know. I'll talk to Pearl and Lucy and get back to you, if that's all right."

"For that money, I could dress each of you well. Maybe for the Story Challenge, even."

Mindy stared but didn't reply.

"Well, think about it, anyway." She started to turn back to the script and halted. "Would you guys be open to another research job? I have an idea, but it will depend on what I find here."

Mindy shrugged. "I guess. Yeah, sure."

Joanna knew this was as enthusiastic a "yes" as she was going to get. "I'll be in touch."

Mindy left, and the store was quiet again. Joanna flipped through her record albums and pulled a June Christie record from its sleeve and set it on the turntable. This would be the perfect soundtrack. As Christie's languorous voice filled the room, Joanna unwrapped the package from the library.

Two women entered the shop, chatting about a mutual friend. Joanna greeted them, and when they said they were "just looking," she returned to the script.

It was a fat bundle of typewritten pages bound with two brass fasteners and a manila cover. *Starlit Wonder* said the title page in capital letters. "Sipriano Productions presents" was typed above the title, and "by Peter Blackburn" was typed below. "UCLA Collections" was stamped in red in the upper right corner, above a handwritten catalog number. In the lower left corner was typed the director's name.

"Excuse me, but do you have this in a bigger size?" The customer held up a ruffled silk skirt, one of the 1970s pieces Joanna was experimenting with selling. Some customers lifted the hangers of these clothes in disbelief, saying things like, "The principal's secretary wore this when I was in high school." The younger crowd was into it, though, and even brought photos of Stevie Nicks and asked about poet's sleeves.

"Everything we have is one-of-a-kind," Joanna said. "I do have a dress by the same maker that's a little bigger." Regretfully, she closed the script. It would have to wait until tonight.

That night, she sat in bed with the script for *Starlit Wonder* open in her lap. The rain pounded on the roof and streamed through the gutters. After she'd closed Tallulah's Closet, she hadn't had a minute to crack open the script. Now, dinner and chores behind them, Paul lay asleep next to her. Thankfully, he'd always been a heavy sleeper, and when a book kept her awake past his lights out, her reading never bothered him.

The script was as engrossing as any murder mystery. As she read, terse stage directions and setting descriptions unrolled the story as clearly as if she were watching from the front row of a screening room. Despite the Busby Berkeley title, *Starlit Wonder* was classic film noir. She wished she could see the characters in their Edith Head-designed costumes.

The story opened with a brother and sister unpacking their bags in their furnished garden apartment. They were in Hollywood. The brother placed his portable typewriter on the kitchen table and announced that his career as a novelist was behind him. From now on, he'd be known as a screenwriter. The sister asked him to write her a role and to make it a big one, preferably with a grand love affair and a happy ending. At this point, the script commanded the sister to look wistfully out the window.

It didn't escape Joanna that the story could have been about Bradley and Mary Pat Stroden. So far.

Starlit Wonder picked up its pace almost immediately. While the brother smoked cigarettes and pounded away at the typewriter, the sister encountered a movie producer in a "meet cute" scene at a pet shop. The sister left with a puppy and the producer's business card. Soon, one of the studios took her on. At the same time, her relationship with the producer flourished.

Until it didn't. Halfway through the script, the producer seemed to have an abrupt change of heart and telephoned the sister to break off their relationship. The sister refused to accept it. While a storm raged through the city, the producer drove through the city to the sister's house in Pasadena, where she had settled once she had her own income. The sister thought he'd come to reconcile, but he stabbed her, ransacked her apartment to make it look like a burglary, and left.

The story's tension kept Joanna turning the pages until the second death, a poisoning. The brother pinned the murder on the producer and was determined to punish him by poisoning his afternoon whiskey. The brother didn't live to feel the satisfaction of revenge, because on his way home, distracted, he'd been hit by a car and killed.

Well. She'd always appreciated film noir more for the style than the tortured plot lines.

But, a second murder, a poisoning. The script rested against Joanna's knees. Bradley Stroden had been poisoned. Coincidence?

She set the script on the nightstand and took up the photocopies of newspaper articles Mindy had ferried from the library. The first was from the *Pasadena Star-News* in 1953, two years before *Starlit Wonder* was filmed. It reported that Brigid Blackburn had been stabbed and killed at her home. She was survived by family in Nebraska and by her brother, novelist and screenwriter Peter Blackburn. The police determined she'd had the bad luck to surprise a burglar. Joanna wondered where the Big Sip had been that night and if the police had even bothered to check.

The next clipping was Sipriano's obituary, dated 1965. He'd died of a massive coronary. No poisoned whiskey. No murder. Sipriano's death had merited two photos. One, a close-up of the producer, probably a studio portrait, showing a fleshy-cheeked, dark-haired man with charisma that shone even through a photocopy of newsprint. The other was a photo of the funeral. A woman in a black coat and hat with a veil stood near a flower-heaped casket. He'd left a widow, Meredith Sipriano, and several children.

Joanna laid the photocopies on top of the script and folded her hands over her lap. It was conclusive. Luke couldn't have blackmailed the producer, because the producer was long dead. Yet she was sure Luke was blackmailing someone. Assuming that *Starlit Wonder* was the hot button, who stood to lose the most from having the film made public?

Sipriano's wife topped the list. If Sipriano did have an affair and murdered his mistress, his wife would want it hushed up. From what Callie Rampton and Mary Pat had said, she was possessive to a fault. She'd never want her dead husband's name besmirched. Peter Blackburn also needed to be tracked down. In fact, everyone involved with the movie merited research.

She took in her small bedroom's dresser topped with a mannequin's bust draped in necklaces, the chair with Paul's work shirt dangling from it, the 1920s painting of a young woman in a dropped-yoke green dress. The bedside light barely touched them with its yellow glow. Outside, the rain continued its strumming, but in here she was warm and dry.

And safe. Her life was settled, content. They hadn't heard from the police. She didn't know if Roscoe had found another copy of the memoir or had wormed anything out of Mary Pat about Gene and the Greffulhe jewels. That shoe had yet to drop. Tonight, though, her life was peaceful.

But the rest of the world wasn't so calm. Anger, jealousy, and greed sparked people to do all sorts of gruesome things. They ruined lives, including their own. Just as in *Starlit Wonder*.

She clicked off the lamp. Hopefully, the Book Bunnies had a few hours on their hands.

Chapter 26

By the time Joanna and Paul awoke the next morning, Uncle Gene was gone. He'd left a hazelnut loaf cake and a note on the dining room table. "Won't be home for dinner. Love, Uncle Gene."

"It's like he knows the memoir rats him out," Joanna said, tossing the note back on the table. She pulled aside the barkcloth drapes and opened a window. The sky was nearly blue enough to taste, and the rain-scented air smelled better than any perfume.

"If it did, it doesn't matter now that it's disappeared. This cake is really good, though." Paul had cut a thick slice and was eating it standing at the table.

"I hate to ask Mary Pat if Roscoe got a hold of the memoir somehow, but I suppose I should." Reluctantly, she turned from the window. "I'll make coffee." She pushed up her kimono's sleeves and passed through to the kitchen. "That cake looks homemade. I wonder where he's been? I thought he and Melba were on the outs."

"Maybe just a stalemate." Paul wiped crumbs from his fingers. "We know he's been somewhere with an accomplished pastry chef and enough baked goods that he was willing to leave some with us."

"Know any bakeries run by crime rings?"

"Now, that's an idea." He pulled out a chair and stretched out his legs.

The day was already beginning to heat up, and Paul hadn't bothered to put on a robe, but sat shirtless in boxer shorts. It was amazing how quickly Joanna had become used to having a half-naked man sitting around. When she'd chosen 1940s hibiscus-print linen to upholster the dining room chairs, she'd never considered this kind of occupant.

Kettle on, she pushed her fingers through his hair and kissed the top of his head. He wrapped his free arm around her waist. "What time do you have to be at the job site?"

"I'm milling a few pieces in the shop this morning. What about you? Is Apple working today? You were up late."

She slowly detached herself and crossed to the kitchen to spoon ground coffee into a French press. "She has today off."

"Was the script as good as you'd hoped?"

"It was a noir-ish story with a tortured hero who dies in the end. If what I hear is right, the main plot mirrors a real life murder."

"Did the newspaper articles help?"

"They did. The newspaper said that the screenwriter's sister, an actress named Brigid Blackburn, was killed when she confronted a burglar. If *Starlit Wonder* reflects what really happened, then Brigid was having an affair with David Sipriano. When Sipriano wanted out, Brigid threatened to tell his wife, so Sipriano killed her." She pulled two mugs from the cupboard. When she'd lived alone, she drank from dainty tea and coffee cups in a mix of patterns. With Paul, it had seemed right to keep an eye out at thrift shops for handmade ceramic mugs in organic shapes. She liked the change.

"You said the tortured hero dies in the end."

"That part is make believe. In the script, Sipriano is poisoned by his lover's brother. In real life, he died of a heart attack."

"Are you going to tell the detective?"

"I could." She'd thought about it. "I'm not sure he'd care, though. I mean, a movie from sixty years ago? A movie that was never even released to the public? It's a stretch. He wasn't even interested in the memoir until he found out someone had kept it from him. He says he's all about solving a homicide by looking at who had the means to kill. Not by motive."

"But you want to get to the bottom of the motive."

Something in his tone of voice made her turn around. He didn't want her fooling around in this murder case. She knew it. But he accepted it. Maybe she wasn't so bad at this marriage thing after all. She was being honest with him, and he was listening.

"Yes. I do. How do you feel about that?"

"I'd feel a lot better if you talked to the police about what you've learned. Let them take care of anything risky."

She smiled. "Thank you. I'll call Detective Roscoe. It can't hurt."

He sat up and leaned forward. "Besides, there are the dresses. You need to stay in touch with Stroden's sister. No telling if she'll decide to sell."

Joanna poured boiling water over the coffee grounds. "You're right. You should have seen the gold evening gown. Silk across the bodice, but a chiffon skirt so soft it would make a baby's bum feel like sandpaper." Remembering, she sighed. "Will you cut me a slice of the cake?" On second thought, she glanced at the clock. "Better not make it too thick. Maybe Roscoe will meet me for breakfast."

Paul complied. As he laid the slice on a plate, he said, "Maybe the detective can tell you whether the jewels made it back to their owner."

"Good point." Some things she might not want to know.

*
**

Detective Roscoe refused Joanna's invitation to breakfast, but said lunch was all right. They made a date for Fuller's Coffee Shop. Mary Pat and Callie had both mentioned the diner as somewhere Bradley Stroden regularly ate. If nothing else, Joanna could sit for a while and soak in the atmosphere. Maybe it would inspire her. If luck held, she might even run into one of Stroden's friends.

Fuller's was that kind of place. It seemed to have emerged from the earth the same time Portland's first resident pitched camp, and it had hummed along in a miasma of hash browns and thin coffee ever since. The coffee shop was a true lunch counter. It had no tables — simply a snaking of counter fronted with vinyl-topped stools bolted to the floor. At Fuller's, to read the menu was to cross the portal to a world where the Monte Cristo reigned supreme and the waitress had your prune juice and oatmeal ready before you sat down.

Joanna set her purse at her feet and flipped over the coffee mug in front of her. The waitress filled her cup without asking and pulled over a dish of single-serve creamers.

"Know what you'd like?"

"What do you recommend?" Joanna didn't miss the waitress's quick once-over that pegged her as a newbie.

"I'll leave you with the menu." She slid a laminated sheet next to the coffee cup and crossed the counter to greet a man in a well-worn John Deere T-shirt.

"You might try the chicken fried steak," the man sitting to Joanna's left said.

"Which one?" the woman to his left asked. "The chicken or the beef?"

"They have chicken fried steak that's chicken?" Joanna said.

"Oh, Fuller's got laughed at when they put it on the menu," the man said. "But they say it outsells the beef version two to one."

The waitress returned. "Decided yet?"

"I'll have the chicken fried steak," Joanna said. "The one with chicken."

"Coming up." The waitress snatched up the menu and took a pitcher of iced tea to the far counter. A fan above the kitchen rustled a calendar near the cash register.

Joanna turned to the man. "Do you eat here often?"

The woman next to him snorted. Her skin was aged and colorless, but her eyes shone mink brown. "Is every day considered often?"

"How else am I going to keep my cholesterol numbers up?" the man said.

"I wonder if you ever met Bradley Stroden. He used to come here."

"Bradley." The man shoveled pancakes into his mouth. Once he'd swallowed, he said, "It's been a while. Used to come in most every day for lunch, what, Linda? Twenty years ago?"

"Twenty, thirty," she said. "When he had the studio next door. Why? You know him?"

Good grief. If they'd been eating here that long, it was a miracle they weren't trailing oxygen tanks. "A bit. I have a vintage clothing store. I know he used to work for Edith Head." In response to their blank looks, she added, "The Hollywood costume designer."

"Bradley loved his dresses," the woman said. "You should be talking to Howard. He's the movie man."

"Best boy," the man said.

"Whatever that is," his friend added.

With one hand, the waitress slid a platter of beige and brown food in front of Joanna while snatching a ticket from the rounder in front of the cook with the other.

"Does Howard come here?" Joanna asked. She'd heard his name, she was sure, if not from Mary Pat than from Callie.

"He's right over there."

Joanna followed the man's finger to a plump, bald man making short work of a stack of toast and a yellow mound of scrambled eggs across the room. He wore suspenders marked with inches like a yardstick.

She was figuring out how to approach him, when the man in the John Deere T-shirt said, "Hey, Howard. Get your plate and step over here. Lady wants to talk to you about the movies." He pushed away his plate and stepped down from the stool. He hitched up his pants, which, despite regular diner meals, were loose. "You can have my seat."

Howard didn't need a second invitation. The paper napkin tucked into his collar as a bib fluttered as he carried his food to the seat next to Joanna's. "You a fan of old movies?"

Joanna recalled Callie asking her almost exactly the same thing. "Well, yes. A fan of the costuming, especially. Did you know Bradley Stroden?"

"Eat up," Howard said, nodding at her platter. "The gravy's nasty when it cools." He laughed, a classic *hee hee hee*.

Joanna obeyed. The chicken fried steak's skin was crispy and salty, and the gravy was rich with mushroom-like flavor. "Delicious."

"So much better than the beef one." He pondered that a moment while he tore off a corner of his toast with his teeth. "Yes, I knew Bradley. Poor man. At least he went quickly. Or so it sounded, anyway. Murder." He shook his head. "Still can't believe it."

"You must have known him from the old days in California."

"And here." He placed a business card on the counter between them. "Handyman Howard," it read. "No problem too big or too small."

"Thank you, I'm Joanna." She had her own resident handyman, lucky for her.

"When I had a job downtown, I used to drop by the studio or meet Bradley here," Howard said. "Now I live in a condo in the Pearl." He looked out the window as if seeing the block for the first time. "Isn't it nuts? Neighborhood used to be all warehouses. Now it's full of nose-in-the-air condos." He shook his head. "Who'd have believed it?"

"The city has changed so much."

He applied himself again to his scrambled eggs. "No joke. I got myself a job in one of the buildings, though, with a rent-free apartment thrown in. I tried to convince Bradley and Mary Pat to sell their pile on the hill and come join me, but they weren't having any."

Joanna couldn't imagine Bradley Stroden giving up his Memphis sofa suite or antique ceramics to pare down to what would fit into a condominium. "I wonder, when you were both in Hollywood, did you happen to be around when *Starlit Wonder* was filmed?"

Howard choked on his eggs. He gulped ice water and cleared his throat. "*Starlit Wonder*?" His voice came out high-pitched. He coughed. "*Starlit Wonder*?" he repeated, this time more clearly.

"Yes. Mr. Stroden told me he had a story about the film in his memoir."

"He did, did he?" Howard tapped his fork on the counter before dropping it on his plate. "I guess it's all right now. But, still. I'm surprised."

"So, there is a story. I talked with Callie Rampton, and she said the movie was about a real-life murder."

"Callie's talking now, too, huh?"

Joanna nodded once but didn't speak. She willed him to continue.

"You know, I told Bradley that story in the first place. Made him promise to keep it secret. He always did love a good piece of inside news."

"Was it the screenwriter? Did you hear it from him?"

"I did. Barely knew the man. As best boy, you get thrown into lots of situations. The director sent me out to deal with a lighting problem, and I ran into the screenwriter behind the set. That was strange all by itself."

"The screenwriter wasn't usually on the set?"

"Everything okay here?" the waitress asked.

"A-okay, Barbie," Howard said.

She splashed coffee in their cups before moving on.

"Nope. It's rare you see them. Blackburn was sitting where he could hear but not see and seemed to be mouthing words along with the cast. Strangest thing I've ever seen." He shook his head. "On the verge of tears, even. "

Breakfast forgotten, Joanna stayed silent, letting Howard relive the moment.

"I asked him if he was all right. He said just one word. 'Brigid.'"

"Brigid," Joanna repeated. "That was his sister's name."

"Uh huh. That's when he told me what he said was the real story behind *Starlit Wonder*. Which was basically the story of his sister's murder. With the ending changed, of course. The movie ended with the producer drinking poison. Big Sip—that's what we called him—"

Joanna nodded.

"—died of a heart attack years later. The poison bit must have been a threat. Part of Blackburn's revenge."

She lowered her voice. "Howard, if I were you, I wouldn't tell anyone about this story."

"I haven't. Until now. Well, I told Bradley, but that was fifty years ago."

"I have a hunch Mr. Stroden was murdered because of it. Be careful."

"No kidding. Because of *Starlit Wonder*?"

"Someone might want to bury that story for good. I'm not sure who." She poked at her breakfast. "Callie said that the Sip was a real womanizer."

Howard snorted. "She should know. She was married to the guy."

Joanna's eyes widened. "Married to him? She didn't tell me that."

Howard nodded beyond her. "Hey, that gentleman seems to be looking for you."

Joanna spun on the stool to face the door. In came Detective Roscoe.

Chapter 27

"Joanna?" the detective said. "Looks like you've already eaten."

Half of her chicken fried steak was left on the platter. Howard had been right. The congealing gravy wasn't the delight it had been half an hour earlier.

"Yes, but—"

"I guess I'll be getting on with my day. Got a water heater acting up in unit sixty-two." Howard stood and pulled the paper napkin from his collar.

"You don't have to leave. You were telling me about Callie Rampton and the Big Sip."

"Not much to tell there. Nice to meet you, Joanna." He proffered a plump hand and shook Joanna's fingers like a pump handle. Detective Roscoe stepped aside to let him leave.

There went her scoop.

"To tell the truth, I'm glad you already had a bite," Roscoe said. He lifted his panama hat, smoothed his wild frizz, and clamped the hat back on. "Wife has me on a low-carb diet." He pulled a sealed baggie of what looked like roast beef and nuts from his pocket. "She even packed my lunch. Would you mind walking while you fill me in? I have about twenty minutes before I'm due back at the office."

Joanna paid her bill, passed up the peppermints at the cash register, and emerged onto the Pearl District's hot streets. "Do you have a direction in mind?"

"How about toward Powell's?" He pointed toward the bookstore three blocks away. "Now, what's on your mind?" As they stepped off the curb, he rolled up a slice of beef and tucked it in his mouth.

"Have you had any luck finding Bradley Stroden's memoir?"

"Not yet. We turned the house upside down but couldn't find a paper copy. We have his computer, though. The techs are working it over. Why?"

Which meant no fingers pointing at Gene. At least, for the moment. "Last night I read the script for *Starlit Wonder*."

"The movie you keep talking about. And?"

She paused at the intersection to let a Volkswagen bus pass. Thank goodness a few of Portland's old hippies remained. "One of Mr. Stroden's friends, Callie Rampton, said the movie reflected a real murder. In Fuller's, I was just talking to a guy who says the screenwriter did it to avenge his sister, who was murdered by a producer, the same producer who funded *Starlit Wonder*."

Roscoe pushed open the doors at Powell's, letting Joanna enter first. She took a deep lungful of cool air.

"So, this producer might have got wind that Stroden was going to blow the cover on him?"

"That was my first thought."

"Your first thought." Roscoe tucked his hat under an elbow. Wet spots spread from his armpits. "What was your second thought, pray tell?"

"The producer died about twenty years ago," Joanna said reluctantly.

Roscoe pursed his lips together. "So, that's that. Was that all you had to tell me?"

"I thought it might help. Might give you some sort of lead."

"Mind if I stop by the Sci Fi section?"

"No. Of course not." Joanna's interest was piqued now. She would have pegged him for military history or something like that.

They passed through one massive room lined with bookshelves and as large as most entire bookstores, climbed a few steps, and emerged into mysteries and science fiction.

"Thank you for the update, Joanna, but at this point, it doesn't matter. Even if the producer were still alive, and even if we could find an old cold case that matched this movie, we don't have the memoir. Without knowing that the memoir had a juicy section on this movie, we've got nothing. See?"

"But—"

"Think about it. What would a judge say? 'Hi, your honor, there's this movie, see, that was never released, that someone says might reflect a real murder that might have been in a memoir, we're not sure, and might have been a motive for killing Bradley Stroden and his secretary.'"

Put that way, she had to admit it wasn't very compelling. Yet every fiber of her body told her something was there. Too many people had secrets about that film. Stroden's own sister thought so.

"Ah, here it is." He pulled a fat novel with space ships on its cover firing orange-tailed missiles. "Give me outlaws in space any day over the kind on the streets. Now, if that's all, I'll head back to the office."

"Is there anything else I should know about the case?" If Roscoe didn't take her information on *Starlit Wonder* and run with it, there was nothing she could do. Nothing but a little more research, that was. Before she went home, she'd check out the shelves of old fashion books upstairs. She'd been looking for a good overview on Balenciaga.

"Since you're not on the case, the answer is no." Roscoe shook her hand and turned for the cashier. He took only a few steps before turning to face her again. "Joanna. I almost forgot—I do have some news for you."

"Yes?"

"We found the Greffulhe jewels's owner, Aimee Miller."

"Oh. That was fast." Images of a half-drunk woman decked out in emeralds filled her imagination.

"It took no time at all. She's in India, working for an organization that ministers to unwanted animals."

"Was she happy to get her jewelry back?"

"Ecstatic. She told us to send it to her lawyer. She plans to sell it and donate the proceeds to the cats of Calcutta."

*
**

At Tallulah's Closet, Joanna went straight for the telephone.

"Mindy?" Joanna was surprised she'd answered. She had the idea that most people texted these days and might return a call after listening to the caller's message—or not.

"I knew it was you," Mindy said. "No one else would call. Even my mom texts."

"Good for her. Listen, remember how I asked if you had time for more research?" Joanna smiled at a customer who'd wandered over from the cafe across the street with a box of leftovers. "I mean, if your mom says it's okay."

"She's always trying to get me to work. Babysit, mostly. I'm not great with kids," Mindy said.

Fancy that. "Well, you're terrific with research, and I need a few people checked out."

"Does this have to do with the stuff I brought you?"

"Exactly. I want to know what's happened with the movie's cast, director, and producer." No one else was listed on the script. "Does that sound like something you could do?"

"I guess."

The customer set her greasy box on a stack of pristine gloves. This was becoming way too common a problem. Thanks to the cord on the shop's princess phone, this time Joanna couldn't both talk and tactfully move the box to the counter. She tore her eyes away and prayed the box didn't leak. "Does that mean yes?"

"Yes," Mindy said. "We're meeting at the library again today. The Book Bunnies, that is. I guess we could do some research for you."

"When do you think you'd be finished?"

Mindy sighed, as if noting and dismissing Joanna's desire for speed. "This afternoon, I guess. Is that soon enough for you?"

"That would be great." They talked about an hourly rate for the Book Bunnies' work. "Or, twice that for trade," Joanna reminded her, trying not to be pushy. She'd get Mindy out of that coat yet.

Chapter 28

Still chewing over Gene's problem at the end of the day, Joanna was headed to the door to pull in the Tallulah's Closet sandwich board when the Book Bunnies arrived, galloping like colts to the entrance.

"Are we too late?" Mindy said.

"You're here," Joanna said, surprised.

"That's kind of obvious," the one with the short black hair and equally black attitude said. Pearl.

"I mean, it's six o'clock. Shouldn't you be home at dinner or something?"

"I thought you wanted background info on the list of people you gave me," Mindy said. As a concession to the heat, she'd undone her topcoat button.

"Well, yes. You already have it pulled together, huh?"

"Child's play," the third girl, Lucy, said.

"As for dinner, we thought you might buy us nachos at Dot's," Mindy said. "I told mom we were working for you. She thinks we're ironing or something."

Joanna looked at the girls. They stared back earnestly. Lucy had a laptop under her arm.

"Okay. Let me leave a message with my husband not to expect me home right away."

A few minutes later, they filled a booth at Dot's. The 1970s amber pendant lights shone dim against the black-flocked wallpaper hung with knock-offs of Margaret Keane's saucer-eyed urchins. Scrawny guys with beards played pool in the bar to a soundtrack of *Heartbreak Hotel*. A waitress in a T-shirt covered with pastel-colored cat heads ambled over.

"Two orders of nachos, please," Joanna told her.

"Three," Pearl said.

"They're huge," Joanna said. "One order could feel a whole family."

"Three is good," Mindy told the waitress. "And fries."

Joanna sighed. "And a martini. A big one."

"I wish they had bubble tea here," Lucy said.

"Yeah," Pearl agreed.

"Well, they don't."

"Then we'll take milkshakes," Mindy said. "Two chocolate, right, Pearl? And a strawberry."

When the waitress left, Joanna laid her palms flat on the table. "What did you find?"

Mindy turned to Lucy. "You read the notes."

Lucy opened the laptop, illuminating her fair skin with a bluish glow. "This was kind of an old movie. We had to, like, find super old newspapers."

"Online," Pearl added.

"Lots of obituaries."

"Of whom?" Joanna asked.

"Hold on. We saved it all." Pearl held up a small plastic thing on a short cord.

"What's that?" Joanna asked.

"See, I told you," Mindy said. "She's hopeless." Then, to Joanna,

"Don't worry. I printed it all out for you."

Joanna relaxed. These kids were all right. Give her an honest nerd any day over one of the made-up teens turning their insecurity into tight jeans and a blasé affect—or, as in the case of Athena's Warriors, attitudes of superiority.

"Did you get your crutches, Lucy?" Joanna asked.

"Not yet. Mom said I can have a wrist brace in the meantime, if I want."

The waitress slid a martini in front of Joanna. "Food will be up in a moment."

"What about the milkshakes?" Lucy said.

"Hold your horses, hon."

"First, the actors," Mindy said, reading the laptop's screen. "The main guy, the one who played the producer?" Mindy continued. "Dead. Along with the movie's real producer. I already gave you that obituary."

"What about the one who played the starlet?" Joanna asked. "The murder victim."

"Dead."

"And the one who played the brother—the murderer—who killed the producer for killing his sister?"

"Whoa." The waitress appeared with a pitcher of water. "Heavy conversation for a bunch of kids."

"Not as heavy as this food will be in their stomachs." When the waitress left, Joanna asked, "The brother, then?"

"Dead," Mindy said.

"Basically, they're mostly dead or living in retirement homes except Callie Rampton and one more person," Pearl said. "The guy who was best boy. Whatever that is."

"Howard. I met him yesterday, actually," Joanna said. "He told me something interesting about Callie Rampton that you might not have followed up on—"

"That she used to be married to the producer?" Pearl said. "The gossip columns ran a notice when they divorced. He took up with an actress, Meredith Hamm, and married her out of the blue. The columnist said something about a 'Hamm sandwich.' What do you think that means?"

"Ask your mom." Joanna filed that information away. Callie seemed to be the "live and let live" type, but she might still harbor bad feelings toward Sipriano and his family. And, potentially, Mary Pat.

The nachos arrived, taking up most of the table space. Mindy snapped the laptop shut and tucked it beside her to make room. The girls busied themselves scooping tortilla chips into guacamole and sour cream.

"Mom never lets us have these at home," Pearl said.

"Make sure you get lots of fiber tomorrow," Joanna said. She leaned back and sipped her martini. Cold and dry. Perfect.

"Basically, we copied everything, except for the stories about the producer's wife's garden. She won a lot of prizes for her roses."

"What did you find on her? She's still alive?"

"Meredith Hamm Sipriano," Mindy read. "We looked her up like you asked. When her husband died, she tried to sue everyone." She looked up. "Gossip columns. She's married to a Lutheran minister now. Lives in Santa Barbara."

The pastilles that killed Bradley Stroden were mailed. They could well have been mailed from California. "Do you know what the widow is doing now?"

"I told you, she's living in—"

"No, I mean right now. As in today." The Book Bunnies seemed to have amazing research powers, but this might be asking too much.

Pearl pulled the laptop to her. "Let me do this." She wiped her fingers and went to work on the keyboard while Lucy and Mindy hoovered their milkshakes with straws. "Got it."

"Facebook?" Lucy asked. "Old ladies love Facebook."

"Watch it, there," Joanna said.

"What?" Mindy said. "My aunt uses Facebook, and she's almost forty."

"Here she is. Meredith Caldwell. That's her name now," Pearl said. "She even posted a video. Look. She's at some kind of spa in Arizona."

Pearl turned the screen to Joanna. A woman reclining on a patio lounger waved her arms and talked. The sound was too low to hear, but it didn't matter. She wore large sunglasses and a floppy-brimmed hat, and Joanna caught the edge of a bandage near her temple.

"That sure is green grass for Arizona," Pearl said. "And look at the flowers."

"You don't go to an Arizona spa for the desert," Joanna said.

Joanna's martini wasn't even half finished, but the platters of nachos now showed nothing but a few loose strands of cheddar, and the milkshakes were mostly drained. These girls could teach locusts a thing or two.

So, the Book Bunnies had uncovered nothing she could use. No new leads at all. She looked at the girls over the rim of the cocktail glass. Mindy was buttoned up tight in her coat. For her sake, Joanna was grateful for the air conditioning at Dot's. Pearl had forgotten her world-weary sneer and was pulling a piece of cheese off the nacho platter. Lucy had attempted lipstick. The center was worn off from their labor over the nachos, and the edges had never been straight.

Maybe all would not be lost.

"The Story Challenge is tomorrow, right?"

"Yeah," Pearl said.

"Still thinking about something to wear?"

*
**

"All right," Joanna said as she locked the door behind them. "Tallulah's Closet is closed for business—except for you. What looks good?"

Without waiting to hear the rest of what Joanna had to say, Pearl went straight for a rack of blouses. "Why did you want all that information, anyway?"

"Because of that dead guy on the hill, dope," Mindy said. "Bradley Stroden."

"It's true. I was there when he died." Would Mindy take off her coat at last? She didn't seem too interested in looking at clothing.

"Can I have these?" Pearl held a zebra-print T-shirt with dolman sleeves, leopard pants, and a wide cheetah-print belt that would sit low on her hips. Joanna had hung all three items in different corners of the store, but like a beagle going after a liver snap, Pearl had unearthed them in seconds.

"You don't think they're a little, oh, Heather Locklear in *Dynasty*?" Joanna asked.

"Who?" Pearl said.

"Never mind. Go try them on. The dressing rooms are in the back."

Lucy had edged toward the floor-length evening gowns. A curious choice for a library literary contest. "But, why all the investigating? You're not the police."

Joanna still wasn't used to Lucy's bell-like voice. "True. I guess I'm just—curious. The man who died was writing his memoir, and he mentioned that *Starlit Wonder* had been controversial, that he had a few secrets to reveal about it."

"So you thought someone killed him because of a movie? They were afraid he'd tell on them?" Pearl yelled from behind the dressing room curtain. She emerged looking hip enough for a *Vogue* spread—not 1980s divorcée at all. "What do you think?" She turned to the mirror. "I could put gel in my hair and wear boots. You don't have any boots, do you?"

"Not anything rock 'n' roll," Joanna said. Now she got where Pearl was going with her outfit. She had a good eye, that one.

"You saw him die?" Lucy asked. She held a 1970s wedding gown with an empire waist.

"You want to try on a wedding gown?" Joanna said. "It might be long on you."

"I don't care." Lucy's burgeoning curves would fill it out fine, but the persistent smudges of dirt on her face and hands and serious demeanor hardly said "bride." "Miyoka wears one like this."

"Anime," Mindy said before Joanna could ask.

Lucy took the gown to the dressing room opposite Pearl's. "It's so pretty. Anyway, tell us about the dead guy."

A woman rapped on the door's glass window. Joanna pointed at the "Closed" sign and waved her away. "He clutched his heart and collapsed right in front of me. We called 9-1-1 and tried CPR, but it was too late. He died at the hospital." Her hands chilled, and she sat on the red velvet bench in the store's center. "The police said he'd been poisoned."

"Gruesome," Mindy said. For a moment, none of them spoke. Unlike the other girls, Mindy had stayed put near the tiki bar, clutching her hands in front of her.

"Is there anything here you'd like to try on, Mindy?"

"I'm not sure."

Encouraging. Not a "no." "Just look around. Really. If anything tempts you, give it a try."

Lucy emerged from the dressing room. As Joanna had expected, the wedding dress was a bit long, but otherwise a good fit.

A smile broke over Lucy's face when she caught herself in the mirror. "I love it! It's so pretty."

"I don't suppose you want a veil, too?" Joanna said, hesitating.

"No. That's ridiculous. Who do you think I am?" Lucy said. She patted the lace bodice. "Can I have this one?"

The dress was priced too high to fall within the girls' research budget, but what the heck. It had been in the shop a while. It would do better out in the world where it could make Lucy happy. "Sure. Change out of it, and I'll wrap it up for you. You're really going to wear it at the Story Challenge?"

Lucy shrugged, but she kept her gaze on the mirror.

Pearl yanked a red knit ensemble from a rack. "How about this, Mindy?"

It was a vivid red coat and dress set by Mamselle Knits that Joanna had despaired of ever selling. She and Apple jokingly called it a "Tallulah's Closet favorite" since it got a lot of commentary, but no one even dared to try it on. The dress had a white yoke and, bizarrely, a red bow tie. Its full-length matching coat had cuff links and wide lapels. It looked like something a circus conductor might have worn during the Nixon administration.

Then Joanna got it. The coat. Mindy liked the coat.

Mindy took her time getting to the rack, but with each step

she showed more interest. The bow tie was witty, Joanna had to admit. Maybe the ensemble had been destined for a middle-schooler all along.

Mindy held the hanger to her chest and turned to the mirror. She nodded. "I'll see what it looks like."

While Mindy tried on the red knit dress, Joanna slipped Lucy's wedding dress into a garment bag. Lucy watched her every move and lovingly hugged the package to her chest. Joanna folded Pearl's various animal print items into a shopping bag, now all stamped by Apple with a red Kelly-style handbag.

"So," Lucy said, "Say the old man really was murdered. And his secretary. What are you going to do if the murderer finds out you're looking into it?"

"How's he going to find out?" Joanna asked.

"You've been asking a lot of questions. If we know you're investigating, why wouldn't he?"

Mindy pushed aside the dressing room curtain and strolled out, hand on her hip. The red knit coat was buttoned tight. She was probably the only middle-schooler in the county swaddled in bright red double knit polyester. "I'll take it."

"Sold," Joanna said. But her brain was working on Lucy's comment. The girl was right.

Chapter 29

After saying goodbye to the Book Bunnies, Joanna returned to Tallulah's Closet. She locked herself in and kept the lights off. The streetlights through the front window stretched the mannequins' shadows deep into the shop. Except for the muffled hum of conversation and music from Dot's, it was quiet now. This might be the most peaceful she'd felt for weeks.

She allowed herself the luxury of a few breaths before returning home. Was Lucy right? Was she putting herself into trouble's path? All she was doing now was looking at old newspaper articles and a screenplay. It was something any college student — or middle-school student, it turned out — might do.

Time to take it to a pro. She closed herself into the tiny storage room at the shop's rear and flicked on the bright bulb overhead.

"Well, Aunt Vanderburgh, what do you think?"

Auntie V looked affronted to hang behind a sponge mop and a buttonless blouse.

Joanna leaned against the opposite wall, next to the shelf that held her coffee-making supplies, and folded her arms.

"It's like this: In the early 1950s, a woman was killed. The official story was that she interrupted a robbery. Her brother was convinced she'd been murdered by her lover. To avenge the lover, who was a film producer, the brother wrote a screenplay that mirrored the murder as he saw it. The producer found out and shelved the movie before it was ever released to the public.

"This year, an assistant costume designer on the film decided to reveal the story in his memoir. Then, both he and his secretary were killed. Got it so far?"

Auntie V was listening but apparently chose not to respond.

"Okay. The assistant costume designer's sister is afraid she might be killed, too, because the murderer will think she's read the memoir. I promised to help her convince the murderer that the memoir would be destroyed if she did me a favor by telling the press that her dead brother had some stolen jewels Gene boosted a long time ago."

If she wasn't mistaken, Auntie V's eyebrows raised a hair.

"You see, Gene simply wanted the jewels to go back to their owner, but he didn't know how to do it without ending up in prison again. Anyway, that's a side problem, but I thought I'd mention it."

Auntie V appeared unimpressed.

"The murderer should be the person who'd stand to lose the most if the movie and its link to a real crime came to light, right? But the producer is already dead." She shifted feet. "And the deal I made about Gene? It doesn't even matter now. Gene's girlfriend is going to make him confess, anyway. I feel so helpless."

At last, Aunt Vanderburgh spoke. *Then walk away. You've done all you can.*

"I could. I could just say 'who cares?' and forget all about this. What do I have to lose now if Mary Pat tells the police the truth about Gene? Besides, she needs a bodyguard, not me."

So, why are you here?

Why was she there? Why was she bothered enough to lock herself in a closet and blather on to a painting when she could be home with her husband — okay, with his uncle, too — eating dinner and joking around?

Joanna stared at the portrait, which now seemed more smug than indifferent.

Joanna knew why she was there. It was because she cared. She wanted to know the rest of the story at least as much as Mary Pat did, even if it put her own life at risk.

*
**

"There you are," Paul said as soon as Joanna opened the door.

The smell of garlic wafted from the kitchen. "Italian bread salad," Gene said, "mostly tomatoes, not bread. I wonder why they call it bread salad?"

"Sounds good," Joanna said. Then, to Paul, "I went to Dot's with some middle-schoolers after the store closed today. You got my message, right? Sorry I'm late."

"I got it. The Book Bunnies?"

She slipped off her 1940s wedge sandals — generally comfortable, but nothing is a walk in the clouds when you're on your feet all day — and rubbed her calves. Gemma loped over to nose at her. "Exactly. Remember the script I was reading in bed? They did some research on members of the cast and crew. I wondered if someone involved with the film had to do with the murders. The first step was finding out who's still alive and where they are." Had she already told him this? "It was just the logical extension of reading the script," she added quickly.

"You won't have to worry about that much longer." Paul pulled out a seat for her at the dining room table. "Want a martini?"

"No, thanks. I had one at Dot's. What do you mean about it not mattering?"

"Mary Pat Stroden has been calling all evening. She wants you to call her back. Says she found the memoir."

Joanna leapt from her chair. "Can the bread salad wait a few minutes?"

"Definitely."

Joanna dialed Mary Pat's phone number, fidgeting with the phone cord as the dial seemed to take ages to return after each digit. The phone rang once, then twice, then three times.

She was just about ready to hang up when Mary Pat answered. "Joanna. I'm so glad you called."

Joanna still forgot that most people had caller ID and didn't go through the charade of "hello?" as if they didn't know who was calling. "I got your message about the memoir."

"Yes! It's such good news." Mary Pat sounded almost giddy.

"What happened?"

"I came back this afternoon from running errands — you know Bradley's memorial service is at the house tomorrow — and I found a trash bag on my stoop with a note attached. The note said 'All is forgiven.'"

"Are you sure it was the memoir?" As she spoke, her mind reeled. Why would the murderer return the memoir at all? Why would he care that Mary Pat knew she was forgiven? It didn't make sense.

"Sure. I was terrified at first. Didn't want to touch it. But the title page of Bradley's memoir was sitting right on top of a bag of shredded paper." She laughed. "I'm so relieved. I can't even tell you. Tonight I might actually sleep."

"I bet you are." Joanna was beginning to wish she hadn't turned down Paul's offer of a martini after all.

"I had thought I might even cancel the memorial service, even though people are coming from out of town. I was so worried. It just didn't feel safe, but now we can go ahead."

"You're sure it's the memoir?" Joanna repeated. "I don't understand why it would be returned like that."

"Why wouldn't it be? That title page was genuine, I'm certain of that. I recognized the purple stain from one of Bradley's pastilles." When Joanna was silent, still taking it all in, Mary Pat added, "You really did help me, and I appreciate it. I just wanted to call to tell you it's over."

"But what about finding out who killed your brother? Aren't you worried about that?"

"The police are handling it." Bradley's demise barely seemed important to her now. "The murderer isn't feeling threatened anymore. He's moved on. I'm safe. I told the police, of course. They took the bag away. Anyway, everything's fine now."

Joanna held the phone to her cheek and turned toward the dining room, where Paul and his uncle stared at her. "Speaking of the police, I suppose Detective Roscoe told you about your brother's memoir? Apparently Luke never gave it to them. He said he was going to follow up with you."

"Oh, yes. He was here. Brought a few gentlemen with him, too. They left empty-handed."

When Joanna replaced the receiver, it was with disappointment. She should have been relieved. Mary Pat was safe. Something didn't sit right with her, though.

"Is everything okay?" Paul had come up behind her and slid an arm through hers. "Are you worried about Uncle Gene because of the memoir?"

She paused. "That's part of it."

An unusually robust sigh came from the kitchen, where Gene had returned and was plucking basil leaves from their stems. "Don't worry about me," Gene said. "I have a plan."

Paul looked at Joanna before releasing her to set the table. "What kind of plan?"

"Are you going to make the apology?" Joanna said.

"I'll make the apology all right." The chef's knife thwacked against the cutting board, and basil fell in slivers.

"Somehow, I'm not relieved," Joanna told Paul.

"Don't worry about it," Gene said.

So. That was it. "Does your offer of a martini still stand?"

Chapter 30

The high school auditorium was crowded. And hot. Joanna flipped open a vintage fan with a painted diorama of Mount Fuji and made what breeze she could, since the school's air conditioning couldn't keep up.

It was starting to sink in that her involvement in the Stroden murder case was over. Mary Pat didn't want her help, Detective Roscoe had made it clear he didn't welcome her butting in, and Paul would rather she stay out of harm's way. Besides, she didn't know what steps she'd take next, anyway.

She'd shift her energy to the shop. Maybe Apple would help her paint it. A deep rose sounded nice. She sighed. Who was she kidding? She was disappointed.

A girl's strident voice caught her attention. It was the know-it-all from the library, from Athena's Warriors. Cool and calm, she strode to a cluster of moms in the first few rows. Joanna spotted some pricy yoga pants and several thousand dollars worth of handbags.

"Hi, Joanna. You came."

Joanna turned to find Mindy and Pearl standing at the end of the row. "I wouldn't miss it. When do you guys go on?"

"We're in the first showdown," Mindy said. She'd unbuttoned a few inches of the red knit ensemble's coat. She might wipe out the competition by sheer force of red polyester alone.

"We'll get slammed and go home," Pearl said, resplendent in animal print. "There's Lucy." Lucy, avoiding eye contact with Joanna, slumped over, the train of her wedding gown trailing behind her. Together, the girls might have made a hip band.

"Where are your parents?" Joanna asked.

Lucy let out a noise that sounded like "humph," and Mindy said, "We didn't tell them."

"At all? You didn't tell them you were competing?"

"Why should we? We'd just be a big disappointment." Pearl picked at a fingernail.

"Where did they think you were all those days you were prepping for the contest?" Joanna asked.

"Why are you here, anyway?" Mindy countered.

"Why else? I wanted to cheer you on."

Lucy met her eyes and allowed a soft smile. Pearl tried to be cool and shrugged.

"Have you been to one of these before?" Mindy asked.

Joanna shook her head. "It sounds like you don't expect I'll be here very long."

"Sure," Pearl said, looking at her feet. "We're on right away. Athena's Warriors have been studying theme and stuff like that. They'll spank us."

"You read the book, right?" Joanna glanced at the program. "*Don't Tell Mom*?"

Mindy shrugged. "Sure, we read it."

The microphone squealed as a middle-aged man with a beard and Hawaiian shirt took the stage. "Welcome to the Story Challenge," he said. "Teams, please go to classroom B to assemble. We'll be starting in just a moment."

The Book Bunnies looked at each other. "We'd better go," Lucy said.

"Yeah," Pearl added.

"Joanna," Mindy said, "thanks for coming."

She and the girl locked gazes. Mindy's earnestness plucked at Joanna's heart. "I wouldn't miss it."

The girls shuffled off, the train of Lucy's bridal gown gathering candy wrappers. Mary Pat would be getting the Stroden mansion ready for her brother's memorial service now. Caterers would be showing up, Callie Rampton would be closing up the stamp shop and setting out a dress, and Howard would be choosing the right pair of suspenders. Bradley's friends from Hollywood—if any were coming—would be turning off the cable TV in their hotel rooms and consulting maps to navigate their way to the bluff-top mansion.

Bradley and Luke's murders hadn't been solved, but the police were on the case. Mary Pat was no longer worried she was in the murderer's crosshairs. Gene was planning to go public with his long ago jewel theft, and whatever happened, he'd be moving out of her and Paul's basement soon.

It's fine, Joanna told herself. Let it go.

"Thank you, everyone," the man in the Hawaiian shirt said. "I'm Principal Spindler, and I'd like to welcome you all to the Story Challenge. Here's how it works. Students from middle schools throughout town read *Don't Tell Mom* and formed teams. All summer long, they've studied the story and met in groups to make sure they know it inside and out."

I'll bet, Joanna thought.

"Today they'll get to show just how thoroughly they paid attention. Now, I'll welcome our first two teams, the Portland Roses and the

Book Bunnies."

The teams of three students each filed on stage and took folding metal chairs facing each other. The lanky boys in the Portland Roses wore soccer uniforms. Maybe they wanted to match. Joanna took in the Book Bunnies' outfits. Even if she didn't know the kids, she knew which team she'd root for.

"Is that a wedding dress?" a woman behind her whispered. "The other one, the one in leopard, looks like Aunt Marcy, don't you think?"

"We'll flip a coin to see which team goes first. I'll ask the team that loses the toss a question about the book. If the team answers it correctly, I'll ask the opposing team a question. When a team answers a question incorrectly, that team is disqualified, and the opposing team has the opportunity to answer it. The winners from this round proceed to the next. Are you ready?"

The Portland Roses nodded vigorously. The Book Bunnies sat, blank-faced. The Book Bunnies won the coin toss, so the boys would get the first question.

"Are you ready?" the principal said. "In *Don't Tell Mom*, what color are the living room drapes?"

The Portland Roses looked at each other. "That's not the kind of question you ask," the tallest of them said.

"Does that mean you can't answer it?"

"We didn't study that kind of stuff," one of the kids said. "I mean, the color of the curtains?"

"Are you passing on this question?" the principal asked.

The pimply boy on the edge folded his arms over his chest and said, "Blue."

Mindy rolled her eyes. Joanna smiled.

"Book Bunnies?" the principal asked. "The answer was incorrect.

Would you like to respond?"

"Yellow," Lucy mumbled.

"Excuse me?" the principal prompted. "Into the microphone, please."

"Yellow."

"With tulips," Mindy added.

"Duh," Pearl said.

"That is correct."

One of the Portland Roses kicked his chair as he left the stage.

The next team, this one two girls and a bespectacled boy, took the seats facing the Book Bunnies, scraping the metal folding chairs against the floor.

As the teams settled, Joanna's thoughts wandered to the Stroden mansion. What was she missing about the murders? If Luke had blackmailed someone while pretending to be Bradley Stroden, it explained both Stroden's and his deaths. But the people with the strongest motives couldn't have committed the crimes. Could the murderer's motive have been something else?

"In *Don't Tell Mom*, the postman mentions a dog having puppies. How many puppies were there, and what were their names?"

The new team answered that one, no problem. Middle schoolers were puppy-savvy, it seemed.

The Strodens again tugged at her brain. Maybe she was all wrong about *Starlit Wonder*. But what other motive might there be? Callie Rampton had hidden her marriage to Sip. Could Bradley Stroden have been poised to reveal something about it that she wanted hidden? Joanna had spent so much time tracking down the screenplay. Perhaps she should have been turning the mansion upside down for another copy of the memoir to uncover other leads.

From the stage, Mindy's voice broke into her thoughts. "She was trapped. That's why Miranda cheated. It was the only way out of camp."

Trapped. Mary Pat had been taken from the man she loved and her life in Hollywood only to be trapped in the mansion with her brother. She'd certainly have the access to poison her brother's pastilles and Luke's coffee. But, kill her brother? That seemed too gruesome to consider. Besides, why now? Why wait all these years?

She clutched the closed fan. Mary Pat inherited. Now she was free. She could sell the mansion and move wherever she wanted. Joanna didn't know what was in the memoir. Maybe—just maybe—Bradley had something on his own sister.

Despite the auditorium's heat, Joanna shivered. No. Mary Pat would never have done this. Would she?

The Book Bunnies had apparently vanquished another team. The moms of the Athena's Warriors sat confidently. One scrolled through her phone.

Mary Pat might have had to kill Luke because he'd somehow figured out that she'd poisoned her brother. He might have tried to blackmail her, too. A fatal mistake.

Detective Roscoe had told Joanna that cyanide used to be a common household poison. The Stroden mansion had been around for a hundred-plus years. Who knew what the garden shed held? Mary Pat would have full access to those poisons.

The memoir, though. Why would Mary Pat shred it and leave it at her own front door? Mary Pat's words came to mind. She had considered cancelling the memorial service. *It just didn't feel safe, but now we can go ahead.* Mary Pat was joyful that she could now go through with the party since the threat of another murder was gone. Why?

Why would she force the situation to hold Bradley Stroden's wake?

The answer sucked the moisture from Joanna's mouth. She clenched her fan so hard that the bamboo snapped. Mary Pat needed to kill again.

On stage, the Book Bunnies looked alert, despite the heat and their earlier lethargy. They were actually having a good time.

"In the refrigerator, next to the cola," Mindy said in response to the principal's question.

"Duh," Pearl added.

Joanna glanced at her scuffed 1930s gold dancing shoes. First she'd dash home and leave Paul a note saying not to expect her home right away. She could explain the rest to him later. Maybe she'd grab some flat shoes, too. Then, it was off to the Stroden mansion.

She'd be damned if she'd let another person die if she could help it.

Chapter 31

She parked Old Blue and squinted down the bluff into the sun. It had started its descent in the west, and warmth radiated from the retaining walls lining the cul-de-sac below the mansion.

The wake had started an hour ago. With this heat, Mary Pat's guests would be inside, at least until night fell. Joanna's plan was to slip into the house and melt into the party. She'd keep an eye on Mary Pat and confront her, if necessary.

She should be able to climb the front steps and enter the back yard through the side gate without running into anyone. She knew where the latch was now, and with the help of the screwdriver she'd had the foresight to tuck into her bag, getting past the garden fence would be easier than last time.

As she'd anticipated, the front steps were clear, and the house was shut tight against the sun, with shades lowered and windows closed. A sprinkler swished nearby. Joanna followed the path to the side gate.

"Looking for Mary Pat?"

Joanna sucked in her breath. "What?"

Carol, the neighbor, leaned over her porch railing in what looked like another brand new easy-breathe tank top with a coordinating blouse open over it. She held a tumbler with ice cubes and clear liquid that might have been water—or a vodka tonic. "You're late to the party. Not that she has any business having guests, not with everyone dropping dead left and right."

"I'm not here for that. I, well, I need to drop something off for Mary Pat," Joanna lied. "I don't want to interrupt her."

"About the investigation?"

"No," Joanna said. "Why?"

The neighbor shrugged. "You might have better luck knocking on the back door. Mary Pat said they were screening a movie in the basement. Come this way—I can help you."

Joanna took the path of stepping stones to the neighbor's porch. Carol held the front door open. Her eyes were bloodshot, and a smear of concealer now only partially covered the beauty mark on her cheekbone next to her eye. Definitely vodka tonic, Joanna thought.

"We'll go through to my yard. We have a neighbor gate."

Carol's house was as spare and as anonymously assembled as her wardrobe. It looked as if she hardly lived there. The sprinkler Joanna had heard earlier rained an arc over her back lawn.

Carol turned off the faucet and pointed to a gate. "Take that. It's unlatched on her side."

Joanna thanked her and crossed the damp lawn to the gate. As Carol had predicted, it opened easily. From the glasses here and there and chairs pulled into the shade, the Strodens' yard had hosted a reception, but it was empty of people now. A cherry red shawl—Callie Rampton's?—draped over one chair. Joanna picked it up. No use letting good silk get bleached by the sun.

Someone called her name. Joanna jumped in surprise. She didn't see anyone.

"Up here." Mary Pat leaned out her bedroom window. "I was just opening windows to get a cross breeze going. Wait. I'll be right down."

So much for melting into the party.

A moment later, Mary Pat's tiny frame filled the sliver she'd opened the French doors. "Honey? What are you doing here?"

Joanna put on her friendliest smile. "I hoped—well, I hoped you would let me join you this evening. After everything we've been through, it didn't feel right, or even respectful, not to come to say goodbye to your brother. Maybe I stay for just half an hour? For closure?" Apple would have appreciated that last bit.

Mary Pat's face softened. "Of course. Come in. I should have invited you in the first place, but I didn't think you'd want to hang out with a bunch of fogeys talking about the olden days." She opened the door further. "Just trying to keep the house cool," she explained and secured the door behind them.

Joanna was keenly aware she could be shut in with a murderer. "Where are the rest of the guests? I thought the house would be full of people." Instead, it was suspiciously calm. No caterers, no spread of hors d'oeuvre, no music.

"I couldn't bear having a large party, so I invited only the people closest to Bradley. After all these years, there aren't many of us left."

Joanna was on high alert. "Carol—the neighbor—said you were screening a movie."

"Oh, yes. Bradley loved to watch the movies he'd worked on. We have quite a collection. But today we have something special." Her smile widened. "You're going to love it. Come downstairs."

The house grew cooler as they passed through the central hall, into the kitchen, and down the stairs to the basement.

"Hello!" Callie pushed up her pair of Edith Head glasses and hugged Joanna. "Oh, you brought my shawl. Would you like a drink?"

"Yes, please." Joanna scanned the room. It was only Callie, Mary

Pat, and Howard. No one else.

"Nice to see you again," Howard said. "Let me make something for you." He patted his comfortable belly, as if he were his own lucky Buddha.

She saw a bottle of Beefeater gin at Howard's elbow. "Can you make me a martini?"

"Abracadabra, you're a martini." He laughed as if he'd invented the joke. Joanna smiled patiently. "Sorry. You bet I can make a martini. They didn't call me the best boy for nothing." Ice cubes clinked into a crystal pitcher. "I brought us a little surprise, too. In a film can." He chuckled again and tipped the gin bottle over the ice.

The screening room embraced the classic red-velvet-drapes-and-tassels scheme. Red velvet upholstered the walls in undulating curves punctuated with pocket lights. The seats—about ten of them—were low-slung 1950s models with black velvet cushions.

Joanna took in the skimpy group. If Mary Pat were the murderer, one of them could be her next victim. "Are you expecting more guests?"

"No. There's a bigger party for Bradley at Fuller's this weekend," Mary Pat said.

"Not many of us left anymore," Callie added. "Would you like a stamp? I had some made up special for today. Look."

Joanna turned the wooden block in her hand and read the backwards letters carved into rubber. "*Starlit Wonder*."

"It's the lettering from the opening credits. You got me thinking about it again. I had a good time laying it out."

"You'll see," Howard said and handed her a Deco crystal coupe with a square-cut stem. Say what you want about Stroden, the man had taste, right down to his barware.

"*Starlit Wonder*," Joanna said. "That's what you brought, isn't it? The actual film."

Howard grinned. "How's that martini?"

She sipped. Ice and juniper and a kick of alcohol. Her gaze wandered toward the windows to the back yard where the garden shed lay, then back to Howard. "Perfect."

"Hee hee hee," chuckled Howard. "I know. And, yes, I brought *Starlit Wonder*. You all haven't seen it since the screening, have you?"

"I've never seen it," Mary Pat said.

"Oh, I'm so excited," Callie said. "I can't wait."

Martini in hand, Joanna glanced over the dim room and velvet-draped screen. "Neither can I."

Chapter 32

Howard cued up the film on a projector at the rear of the room. Mary Pat drew shut the velvet curtains on the narrow basement windows. One didn't close completely, and a sliver of daylight sliced the room's darkness.

"Everyone ready?" Howard asked. "Got your highballs filled?"

People settled into the armchairs. Callie draped her shawl around her shoulders — the basement was cooler than the August afternoon outside. Joanna took a seat near the rear. She'd have the best view of the room from here.

"We're ready. Let her roll," Mary Pat said.

With a flick-flick-flick, the projector sputtered to life. An orchestra's flourish filled the room, and *Starlit Wonder* in big black-and-white letters appeared, exactly as in the rubber stamp.

"I always did have a good memory for graphics," Callie whispered.

"It's in black and white?" Joanna asked. "By the mid-1950s, I'd have thought it would be in color."

"Lots of noir films were shot in black and white," Howard said. "Another martini?"

"No, thank you."

"Hush. Here's Norma. She loved a party, that one," Callie said. She turned to Joanna. "She's the actress who played Brigid."

"Joanna, you'll like that day dress," Mary Pat said. "Edith designed it with a stand-away collar. Remember it upstairs?"

She did. She saw why Head focused on the collar. Norma was slender but low-waisted, and the collar put the focus on the woman's radiant face. The color—all that taupe—made sense now, too. In black and white, it was a good foil for the actress's raven hair and fair skin.

"Whatever happened to her?" Mary Pat asked.

"Last I heard she'd moved to Boca Raton."

Joanna could have added that she'd died a few years ago of breast cancer, but there was already too much death in the room.

"Look, there I am. What a figure," Callie said as her character entered the set. The character waved her arms and said, "Brigid, honey, have you been crying?"

Unsurprisingly, the film followed the script, from the starlet's laments over her ill-fated romance with the producer, to their loving scenes at dinner and their growing relationship. Even though Joanna had read the script, she was swept away by the story, wondering if the producer would ever leave his wife.

The reel flapped to a close.

Howard raised the lights. "Won't be a sec." He pulled the reel from the projector. "Anyone need a refill?"

The words, the lights jerked Joanna into the current day. Her glass was still half-full.

"I'll take another, if you don't mind," Callie said. "Margarita, no salt."

"How about a cola?" Mary Pat asked. "I bought a six-pack especially for you."

"I could get it for you," Joanna said. And make sure it hasn't been tampered with, she added silently. Callie had been married to Sip. This might be enough of a reason for Mary Pat to want her dead.

"Next one," Callie said. "In Bradley's honor, tonight is a two-cocktail evening."

"Do you think — I talked about this a bit with Callie and Howard" — Joanna shot a glance at Mary Pat — "do you think *Starlit Wonder* really did reflect a real case?"

Howard chuckled his signature *hee hee hee*. "I'll say it did." Howard's knowledge could put a target on him, too. Joanna would have to keep her eyes on both him and Callie.

"At least, the Big Sip sure thought so. He put an end to the movie's release like that." Callie snapped her fingers. "We barely got further watching the movie than we are now when he shouted, 'It's over!' and stomped out of the room."

"He really wanted revenge. The screenwriter, that is," Joanna said.

"I think he wanted to clear his sister's name." Callie shook her head. "I'll never forget it. The Santa Ana was really howling the night we screened *Starlit Wonder*. When he threw open the door, it stayed open, and papers blew all over the screening room. One of the crew finally shut the door. We must have sat there in the dark for ten straight minutes before the director said, 'That's it. Everyone go home.'"

"Was the screenwriter there?" Joanna asked.

"He was there all right," Howard said. "Looking pretty proud of himself, too."

"Oh, but Sip. I'd seen him all sorts of ways, but never as angry as then," Callie said.

"Probably terrified of his wife," Mary Pat said.

"I wonder what ever happened to her?"

Joanna knew the answer to this question, too, and asked another one in response. "Are the characters in the movie a lot like they were in real life?"

"The Big Sip was practically a double," Callie said. "I know I was cast for my looks."

"You weren't the only busty blond in town," Howard said.

"As if you cared," Callie said. "Hurry up with that drink."

"In a minute. I've got to get this reel lined up."

"Anyway, yes," Callie continued. "I remember they gave me this awful coral nail polish. You can't see it in the film since it's black and white, but the screenwriter had insisted, said it made it more realistic. The director didn't have to listen to him, but it was easier not to fight it." She readjusted her shawl. "I suppose because we all knew the real story—or thought we did."

"The Big Sip was a wonderful man," Mary Pat said with sadness.

The room quieted. Callie turned to face her. Howard set down the tequila bottle. They all froze, waiting for the next words.

"All he wanted was a quiet life. All he wanted was a home where he could get away from Hollywood." In these two sentences, her voice had fallen from sadness to despair. Tears webbed her powdered cheeks.

"Oh, honey." Callie lowered herself into the chair next to Mary Pat's and draped her arms around her shoulders. "We've all had a rough time lately, you especially. I understand."

Joanna barely made out Mary Pat's words beneath the sobs. "Bradley found out and took me away. Here. That was it." The rest of her words were lost.

"He said he'd take care of you, didn't he?" Callie said. Apparently this story was not news to her. "He was good to me. The Big Sip always took care of his girls."

"It was Meredith, wasn't it?" Howard said. "She chased you out of town."

Mary Pat nodded. Her tears were subsiding. Callie patted her back and returned to her chair. A fresh margarita sat on the side table. Joanna had watched it being made, from splash of triple sec to lime, and it didn't appear tampered with.

"Poor Bradley," Callie whispered.

"I know." Mary Pat's words were hitched by sobs. "He really did want what was best for me."

"Bradley had his quirks, but he was a good man," Callie said. "I'm sorry he's gone. I can't even imagine how you feel, honey."

Mary Pat drew in a long breath and let it go. "Thank you. I lost it there. I just…I guess I shouldn't be drinking."

"It's okay, hon."

Howard cleared his throat. "Let's keep watching. If you're all right with it, Mary Pat?"

Mary Pat took a wavering breath. "I'm sorry. It's all the stress. And that poor girl in the film."

"Do you think he really killed her? Sipriano, I mean." Joanna softened her voice, hoping it would take the edge off of the question.

Mary Pat stared at her so long that Joanna was sure she'd decided not to answer. Then she said, "No." Her voice was stronger now. She turned to the screen. "I'm fine. Let's keep watching."

The film again whirred to life. Joanna half-paid attention as scenes passed by—moody traffic, an impassioned argument between Brigid and her scriptwriter brother, lunch at an L.A. diner.

Yes, Mary Pat stood to gain from Bradley's death, but what did she have now that she didn't have before? She couldn't have sold the house without her brother's consent, but she wasn't hurrying to put it on the market now. Could Joanna have been wrong about her?

But who else had the access to murder Bradley and Luke?

Now they were at *Starlit Wonder*'s last act. The scene was in the Big Sip's living room, and if this was what his real home looked like, life had been good to him. The sunken room was full of low, plush couches and sleek silver lighting. Doors opened to a palm-lined patio. The actress playing the producer's wife strode into the scene, her evening gown swishing around her calves.

"Bradley designed that one," Callie whispered to Mary Pat.

The character put her hands on her hips. "Have you been playing around with that tramp?" she said.

Ouch, Joanna thought. Not the finest dialogue.

"I swear to you, you're the one who matters to me," the producer said.

Something was familiar about the producer's wife. It was vague, but nagging. Callie had said the producer's wife had once been an actress herself. Maybe the casting director had found a double for that starlet, and Joanna had seen one or the other in a movie.

At last they came to the movie's climax, the murder. The room was quiet. Even Callie didn't speak.

On the screen, Brigid and the producer embraced, Brigid wearing the negligee Joanna had seen upstairs. The producer jerked the actress away from him. They shouted. Joanna found herself gripping the chair's edge, her muscles tense.

"I'm sorry," the producer said, gasping. He plunged a jagged-edged knife into the starlet's side, drew his hand back, and stared at the blood.

"All that chocolate syrup," Callie whispered.

"What?" Joanna said.

"They used it for blood in the black-and-whites," Howard said.

"A living nightmare to get out of your hair. You didn't want to be in a gangster flick, believe me," Callie said.

Joanna's breath caught. "You're sure? They used chocolate syrup for this movie, too?"

"Of course."

"Definitely," Howard added. "I must have gained five pounds in Hollywood from fake blood alone."

The negligee from the Edith Head wardrobe. That had not been chocolate syrup. She closed her eyes. The negligee had rust-brown stains. Oxidized. Absolutely not food. Her eyes flew open. Bradley had saved the negligee for a reason.

As she pondered this, the movie continued. The starlet's funeral. The brother thrashed his hand against his steering wheel. Night was falling, and rain slicked the buildings.

Now they were at the producer's house. The man playing the Big Sip looked strong and prosperous. In the scene, his wife straightened his tie. As she laughed, her hair fell back, revealing a beauty mark just to the outside of her left eye.

A mole. Just like the neighbor's mole. Carol. Carol hadn't lived next door long. Carol would have had easy access to the Stroden mansion.

In the film, the screenwriter drove the streets in a fury, rain pounding on the car, the windshield wipers unable to keep up. Still to come was the scene with the poisoned drink.

"Did the producer's wife have a mole by her eye in real life?" Joanna asked.

"What?" Callie swiveled her head toward Joanna. "You ask that now?"

"I don't know," Mary Pat said.

"In fact," Howard said, "she did. Like I said, the screenwriter insisted on every detail. He'd convinced the director it was the only way to bring the film to life. I remember the props gal complaining, because they had to have camellias in the vases even though we were filming in summer and they were out of season."

It was Carol. Carol was Meredith Sipriano. Joanna stood up so fast, she tipped over the table next to her, sending her martini glass to the carpet. She had to call the police.

A quiver in the shaft of light through the crack in the curtains caught her attention. Feet, clad in brand new hiking sandals.

The skin on her back prickled from her skull to the seat of her skirt. And she smelled smoke.

Chapter 33

"Anyone else smell smoke?" Joanna asked. The scent was thickening.

"Maybe it's the projector," Callie said.

"I smell it, too," Howard said.

Joanna threw open the basement door. "We've got to get out of here. It's Carol. The neighbor. She's Meredith, the producer's wife, and she wants to burn the house down with us in it."

That was it. Pretending he was Bradley Stroden, Luke had black-mailed Meredith Sipriano. Luke didn't know what she looked like, though. Both Callie and Mary Pat had mentioned how jealous the Big Sip's wife was. To shut down the blackmailer, she'd moved in next door. That's how the pastilles and Luke's coffee were poisoned, and how the memoir was stolen, shredded, and returned. It was easy. She knew who was home and when. The neighbor gate made access to the mansion a cinch. Roscoe had been right to focus on means all along.

The neighbor also knew they were watching *Starlit Wonder*, and she wanted to make sure the movie was destroyed, along with anyone who had seen it.

"What are you talking about?" Howard said, but he'd stood and dragged Callie up with him. The movie flickered on the screen behind them.

Mary Pat was trembling. "She's right. I hadn't thought about it, but she's right. I told Carol about the movie, that Howard had it. I even invited her to come, too."

Joanna grabbed Mary Pat by the shoulders and pushed her toward the door. "We're going. Now."

Carol—Meredith, rather—might try to keep them from leaving while the house burned. She'd probably start the fire at the exits. They had to hurry.

"Everyone, out!" Joanna said.

They rushed up the stairs and burst into the rear salon. Fire already raced across the deck and darted up the wood framing the French doors. Old growth fir went up like balsa.

"The front door," Mary Pat gasped.

For their age, the guests moved with remarkable speed. They pushed through the central hall to the front door.

"The door's on fire, here, too!" Callie said. Smoke poured through the doorframe.

"The library. Quick," Joanna said, already running toward it. She stopped at the phone and lifted the receiver. The line was dead. "Does anyone have a cell phone? Call 9-1-1."

She threw open the window. On this side, the house hugged the embankment, making it impossible for someone to start a fire here. It also meant a long drop to the driveway beneath.

Howard stuck his head out the window and withdrew it just as quickly. "It's a long way down."

"We don't have a choice," Joanna said. "We're going to have to climb out." She tore the drapes off the window and ripped down the sheers behind them, knotting them into a rope. They'd have to do. "Anchor this to the desk and use it as a ladder." She turned and ran again for the central hall.

"Where are you going?" Mary Pat said. "You can't go in there. The fire's already spread!"

"I have something I have to do. Go. Get out while you can."

Was she completely stupid? Was this a suicide mission? She took the stairs two at a time and ran into Bradley's dressing room. *Quick, quick.* Where was the key?

The smoke was beginning to rise, but she could still breathe. She knew enough not to open the window, because air would only feed the fire. She rushed next door to ransack the desk. Ah, here it was.

Her fingers palsied with adrenaline and nerves. She jammed the key into the wardrobe and bit off a curse. "Turn!" At last, the door opened.

She rummaged through the rack, yanking dresses off their hangers until she got to the negligee. Here was the proof she needed. The silk was soaked with DNA. If she had a say, Meredith would be put away for a long time. That is, if Joanna survived to tell about it. She turned for the hall.

The smoke was now too thick to navigate. Going down the back stairs was impossible. She shut the dressing room door and winced as she shoved the skirt and jacket of a Head-designed day suit under the crack. "Sorry, Edie."

Now she could open the window. She yanked up the sash and leaned out. The cul-de-sac lay three floors below—she was directly over the library.

"Joanna!" Howard stood in the backyard spraying a garden hose at the flames. It had all the effect of spit on a wildfire. Sirens shrieked in the distance. Would they be too late?

She couldn't throw the negligee out the window. It was too light and would catch in the fire. Jumping was impossible, too. Not only was it too high, she'd be jumping straight into an inferno.

She ran into the adjoining bedroom and shut the door to the hall there, too. Smoke closed her throat and burned at her eyes. She ripped the top sheet off of Bradley's bed—good Irish linen, she wasn't too impaired to note—and tied it to a bedpost. She tested the knot. Secure. She could do this.

Now for the bottom sheet. Her yank met resistance. She snapped her head up. Standing at the foot of the bed was Meredith Sipriano, hefting three film cans in one arm and holding the sheet with the other.

"Trapped now, aren't we?" she said.

"How did you get up here?" Joanna held the sheet tight.

"The kitchen door is so old it opens with a skeleton key. Can you believe it?" She yanked the sheet again.

"Let go!"

Surely Meredith couldn't hold the heavy film and the sheet at the same time, but the sheet didn't give. She seemed to have superhuman strength. In the near distance, something exploded, rippling a boom through the house and feeding the flames' roar.

"Why did you have to get involved? You did this to yourself, you know," Meredith-Carol said. She let go of the sheet and flung a canister of film like a discus through the heat-weakened bedroom door. Flames whooshed from the hall.

Joanna backed toward the window, her bundle clutched firmly under an arm. "Why are you doing this?"

"We have a good marriage, me and Sip. No one can take that away. No one." Whether she was yelling from anger or from the need to be heard above the roar of the fire, Joanna couldn't say. "She didn't understand. She had to die."

"He's dead, do you hear me?" Joanna shouted in reply. As she talked, she knotted the sheets together. The rope she'd constructed would give her only a dozen feet's advantage, but she had no choice. She might survive a fall, but she wouldn't live another three minutes in the house. "We're getting out of here. The window."

"No!" Meredith yelled. The remaining film cans hit the floor with thuds barely audible above the flames' thunder.

Pulling her shirt over her mouth to breathe, Joanna grabbed the woman's elbow and yanked her toward the window.

Meredith jerked back. "You don't know what love is! You don't know what a good marriage is!"

"Come on! You'll die if you stay." As soon as the words left her mouth, Joanna understood. Meredith never planned to live through this. "He isn't worth all this. Sip is dead. It doesn't matter if he murdered Brigid Blackburn. You don't have to save his reputation anymore."

Meredith began to scream. At first, Joanna thought it was panic, but she realized the woman was laughing. "Sip? You don't get it, do you? I don't care about that cheating bastard. He didn't kill her."

"What?"

Meredith widened her face in a smile more chilling than any killer's scowl and mouthed, "It was me." She ran for the shattered door and leapt into the hall's pulsing orange glow.

No time to think. Joanna heaved herself out the window with her bundle under her arm and a vice-like grip on the sheet. She gulped air as she lowered herself inch by inch. Her throat burned. She heard nothing but the pounding of blood in her ears and saw nothing but the linen that dug at her palms.

All the while, Meredith's ash-stained face mocked her. *It was me,* she'd said. She'd killed Brigid Blackburn. Her husband was not the murderer. Peter Blackburn and Bradley Stroden had been wrong. Everyone had been wrong.

Down the makeshift rope Joanna climbed until she had no more rope left to give. Her feet dangled, and her arms and shoulders quivered with effort. The drop would be more than twenty feet, straight onto concrete.

She let go. And fell all of one foot, into the iron grip of a fireman. She flopped as she'd seen Pepper do on his more ambitious naps. "Thank you," she whispered as they descended the ladder.

She was handed off to another fireman, then to a paramedic a safe distance away. Above her, the house howled with red and orange flames and fireflies of cinder scattering at its edges. The window she'd crawled out of was now a sheet of fire. She counted five fire engines below the mansion, two of them arcing thick streams of water at the blaze.

"Are you all right?" the paramedic asked. He clipped something onto her finger, then slipped an oxygen mask over her mouth and nose.

She nodded. She pulled the mask away to say that Meredith Sipriano was still in the house, but a glance toward the mansion told her she couldn't have survived.

"What's that?" He pointed at her bundle, still clamped beneath her arm.

For a moment, she'd forgotten about it. "Oh. This is evidence in a murder." She coughed and took another draught from the oxygen mask. The negligee was wrinkled, but the crime lab wouldn't care.

"What about this one?" The paramedic lifted a strapless gold silk gown.

Joanna wiped the grime from her eyes. "Careful. That, my friend, is a masterpiece."

Chapter 34

Joanna felt like a queen. A queen who was a little beat up and smelled like Chicago after Mrs. O'Leary's cow knocked over the lantern, but a queen nonetheless. She was propped up on the couch with pillows and a blanket, and had three men and a dog ranged around her. Paul sat the closest, pressing a damp washcloth to her forehead. The cat didn't like the disruption and had retreated to the basement, where he was probably curled up on Gene's bathrobe.

"So," Foster Crisp said, "The neighbor was the murderer. She was there all along."

"And her real name was Meredith, David Sipriano's widow, right?" Paul said.

"Exactly." Joanna drained half her glass of water and stuck it out for a refill. Cool, pure water had never tasted so good.

"Bradley Stroden's secretary was putting the bite on her, so she rented the house next door to keep an eye on things," Gene said.

"If 'keeping an eye on' means 'killing,' then, yes," Joanna said. "Think about it. It all makes sense. She had full access. Who else would be able to poison the violet pastilles and the letter? Not to mention steal the memoir and return it, shredded, to the front door?"

"Why did she do that?" Crisp asked.

"She wanted Mary Pat to let down her guard and hold the memorial service after all."

"She doesn't have priors," Crisp said.

"Maybe she'd never been pushed to the limit before. Except that once, when her husband might have been tempted to leave her. She took care of that problem." Joanna thought about the negligee, now with Detective Roscoe. "She had no idea another copy of *Starlit Wonder* existed, either. She'd already destroyed the one in the UCLA archives." Joanna was sure it had been she who had stolen the copy. "She had to get rid of this copy, too, and anyone who knew what was in it."

"So she moved next door," Gene said.

"I can imagine her, after she received Luke's blackmail letter, researching Bradley Stroden and trying to figure out how to contain the scandal that would erupt when his memoir came out," Joanna said. "More water, please." She cooled her throat. "She discovered the house next door was vacant."

"I can see why," Crisp said. "The traffic noise is horrible."

"So she rented it and faked a video of spending time at a spa. Now she was in the ideal location to stalk her blackmailer and shut down the memoir for good."

"All along, people had assumed Sipriano killed his mistress," Paul said.

"Even the mistress's brother. He'd pinned the murder on Sip in his screenplay. Meredith was desperate that no one would figure out that she killed Brigid Blackburn all those years ago. All they'd have to do is reopen the investigation into Blackburn's death and track her movements that night."

"The DNA on the nightgown will clinch it, of course," Crisp said.

"So, it's finally over," Paul said. He set the damp cloth aside and clutched Joanna's hand. "I'm not going to lie. I'm glad." He gave her a look that said, "We have some talking to do."

Joanna headed him off. "It's a shame the old house is gone. And the Edith Head costumes — well, most of them, anyway." The gold evening gown would need a careful cleaning, but it had survived. "I wonder…"

"Wonder what?" Crisp said.

"Mary Pat told me that Edith Head had insisted Bradley Stroden take the costumes. Head knew movie blood from the real thing. Do you think…?"

Crisp smiled. "I like it. Not that it matters now."

"I feel that somehow Peter Blackburn knows his sister's murder was solved, even if he'd been wrong about her killer." Joanna set the water glass on the coffee table near her head. At last, she felt calm. Except for one item. "How are things with you, Gene?"

"Have you thought about your confession?" Paul added after a glance at Joanna.

"Oh, with all the excitement, I forgot to tell you about it. It's done. I wrote it all out right here." He pulled a sealed envelope from his back pocket and tossed it on the coffee table. It was fat enough to hold plenty of details and was addressed to *The Oregonian* with a P.O. box as a return address.

Joanna and Paul exchanged glances. "So, you wrote it all out. But you haven't sent it in yet."

For a man pending a return to prison, Gene looked relaxed. Joanna thought he might have loosened his belt a notch, too. Those baked goods were adding up.

"I don't have to. I showed Melba, and we walked to the mail drop together. She asked a few questions, and I told her how, when word got out, my parole officer would tighten the screws and might cite me for hiding evidence, but that my prison term wouldn't be longer than a few years. If I was lucky."

Crisp raised an eyebrow. "Go on," he said in a dry tone.

"Well, I'd opened the hatch to the mailbox, was just about to slip in the letter, and she pulled back my arm. Said the fact that I'd written my confession was enough for her, and, besides, the Greffulhe jewels were where they belonged, anyway. Plus, she has a soft spot for cats."

"Smart woman," Paul said.

"It's true," Gene said. "And a looker, to boot."

"I hope you'll bring her by the house sometime soon. We have a lot of pastries to thank her for."

"We'll both come. I'm leaving soon. Nearly packed. There's a little apartment above the bakery with my name on it."

"What are you going to do for money?" Joanna asked.

Gene looked at Crisp. "Foster said he might have some jobs for me here and there."

Crisp shrugged. "He knows the community. He's a good contact for a P.I."

Joanna reached for Gene's arm. "I'll miss you. I will."

"Oh," Paul said. "One more thing. Apple forwarded it to me. One of the Book Bunnies stopped by the shop."

He showed her the screen of his phone. The Book Bunnies stood holding a trophy shaped like a book. They were all grinning, even Pearl. Joanna pulled the phone closer. Could it be? Mindy had taken off her coat. The Mamselle Knits sleeveless dress showed white arms reaching for the trophy.

Joanna's head fell back onto the couch. Things really seemed to be wrapped up. "What a memorial service that was," she muttered.

"A hell of a finale," Crisp added.

"Truth is," Gene said, "Bradley would have loved it."

The next night, Joanna and Paul sat on the couch, alone. Open windows brought in cool night air and the songs of crickets.

"It's been a while," Paul said.

He didn't need to finish the sentence. Joanna knew what he meant. It had been a while since they'd had the house to themselves with no Gene to feed or to appear in the middle of the night or to tie up the bathroom.

"It has. He was a good houseguest, though."

Paul looped an arm around her shoulders and squeezed them. "Come on, you're glad he's gone."

She laughed. "I'm glad we have the place to ourselves again."

For a few minutes they sat in silence.

Joanna reached for Paul's hand. "I'm sorry I didn't leave you a longer note when I went to the Stroden house yesterday. It felt like an emergency, and I didn't have time to spare."

Paul withdrew his arm and faced her. "You didn't leave me a note. I mean, I knew something was up because you'd come home and changed your shoes to the ballet flats."

"But I did. I wrote it on the pad we keep in the buffet drawer. You know, the one for the grocery list. I left it on the table." She placed a hand on his forearm. "I wanted you to know what I was up to. Like we'd talked about."

He pushed aside her hair and kissed an ear. "Thank you. But I didn't get any note."

As if having the same thought, they both looked at the envelope Gene had left on the table. "Gene left his confession. Do you think —?" Paul started.

"He might have written it on the same pad and tossed aside my note."

Paul leaned forward and picked up the envelope. He handed it to Joanna.

It felt heavy. She squeezed it. "I wonder what he said? I mean, we know the story. I just wonder…"

Paul took it from her. He slipped a finger under the envelope's flap and ripped.

"You can't open that," Joanna said. "It's private."

He shot her a sideways glance. "If I know my uncle, it won't matter. Here."

He pulled out several sheets of paper and smoothed them flat. They were blank.

Joanna's mouth dropped open. She laughed and shook her head. "Honestly. Somebody ought to make a movie about this."

Acknowledgements

Thank you to my writing group—Cindy Brown, Dave Lewis, Doug Levin, Ann Littlewood, and Marilyn McFarlane—for their patience, encouragement, and gallons of herbal tea over the years. Thank you also to Deborah Guyol and Charlotte Rains Dixon for red wine at Noble Rot and lots of encouragement. A big thanks to Michaela Bancud for suggesting the title. Raina Glazener provided the eagle-eyed copy editing.

Liz Gross, proprietress of the Xtabay, the inspiration for Tallulah's Closet, helped to dress the Book Bunnies for the Story Challenge. (If you look good in screaming red polyester, I bet the Mamselle Knits ensemble is still available). Captain Louisa Jones of the Portland Fire Department was immensely helpful in describing what goes down when a Victorian mansion catches fire.

My biggest thanks is to my readers. I am grateful for you every time I sit down at my laptop.